Partners By Design

By Pamela Stone

Partners By Design

Text copyright @ 2013 Pamela Stone
All Rights Reserved

This book is licensed for your personal enjoyment only. This book may not be re-sold or given away to other people. If you would like to share this book with another person, please purchase an additional copy for each recipient. Thank you for respecting the hard work of this author.

Cover Design by Rae Monet

Partners By Design

DEDICATION

As always, this book would have never happened without the help of my two talented Critique Partners, Juliet and Linda. These two ladies have stuck with me through the good and bad times in my career. Also thanks to all my friends and family who enhanced my love of Fort Worth. Wonderful memories of growing up in a unique city packed with history and personality. From the Fort Worth Stock Yards to the cultural museums to the amazing architecture. Thanks Fort Worth.

Partners By Design

Partners by Design

Chapter One

"Somebody pinch me." Savannah followed Mallory up the wrought iron and wood staircase in a euphoric daze. Gorgeous renovated office building. Classy neighborhood full of wonderful old homes. Less than a mile from Texas Christian University. Perfect location for their new interior design business.

Her pulse raced as she calculated the rent into their budget. If they skipped lunches, they could almost afford their half of the two-office suite Mallory had leased.

At the second floor landing, Savannah followed the sharp zing of a nail gun to find a construction crew working on the finishing touches. A guy with a ponytail flashed a grin then returned to staining an office door a rich walnut. Savannah drooled over the scents of fresh paint and varnish.

Mallory traipsed into one of the offices. "Hey, Logan. Wanted to introduce you to my business partner."

The deafening power tool silenced and a man wielding a nail gun turned to face them.

Partners By Design

Logan?

Savannah choked on her own breath. Honest to God, she couldn't suck enough air into her lungs. Logan Reid.

His white tee shirt clung to his broad shoulders like a second skin. She blinked at the line of sweat that accented his pecs, then continued down his hard stomach, and disappeared beneath the waistband of faded jeans. Every nerve ending in her body quivered, just like they had eight years ago.

Logan stood motionless, his face a reflection of her own shock.

Mallory had managed to find the perfect office and she'd contracted to share it with Logan Reid? Savannah couldn't do it. There wasn't an office in Fort Worth that could justify having to face him every day.

"Hello, Savannah."

'Go to hell,' were the first words that came to mind. She swallowed. "You're looking well."

Logan's gaze roved over her body like a physical touch. "You too," he said, but he didn't meet her eyes. Classic guilt indicator.

Mallory frowned. "You two know each other?"

"High school." Logan swung the nail gun to his side and nodded.

Savannah shoved her hair off her sticky forehead. Jeez, it was hot for the

Partners By Design

first of October.

>She searched Logan for any imperfection. Premature balding or a beer gut. She'd settle for a pimple. His shorter hair leaned more toward sandy brown than blond now, but otherwise he hadn't changed.

>Correction. The boy who'd stolen her heart only to tromp it into mush had filled out in all the right places. Not that she had any interest in smooth talking jerks. Not even older, well-toned ones.

>Their eyes met, but didn't hold.

>Savannah peeled her clenched fingers from Mallory's arm. One more flex of tee-shirt-encased biceps and she'd snatch that nail gun out of Logan's hand and nail his butt to the wall.

>"Mallory said we were sharing an office with an architect. You also work on the construction crew?" she asked.

>"Construction foreman. The architect I'm interning with designed the renovation."

>"So you aren't an architect?" she persisted.

>One eye narrowed. "I finish my Masters in December."

>Mallory waved a sunshine yellow tape in the air. "We stopped by to measure the suite and see if our furniture will fit."

>Logan laid the nail gun on top of a tool bag, dug a key from his pocket, and

Partners By Design

tossed it to Mallory. "Knock yourself out. I've gotta finish this."

Walk, Savannah told herself. Just one step, now another. Don't flinch. Don't look back. And for cripe's sake, don't trip.

Mallory led the way to suite twenty-two and unlocked the door. Savannah stumbled in and pressed her palms flat against the wall, squeezing her eyes shut. "You already signed the lease?"

"You wouldn't let me off the phone until I did, remember? You kept squealing, 'It's TCU.' We're getting the coolest location in Fort Worth and for half the rent. How was I supposed to know you had some kind of hot and heavy history with our suite mate?"

Savannah shoved her hair back. Eight damn years! She was over it. She had to be. "He won't hold us to the contract. He can't be any more eager to face me every day than I am to see him."

"Geez, Savannah! What the heck happened between you two?"

"I don't want to talk about this." She'd never mentioned Logan to Mallory. Or to anyone. She'd buried him so deep in her psyche she'd almost convinced herself that the interlude never happened. He hadn't existed.

"We can't afford to pass up this suite over a bad high school romance," Mallory said.

"I cannot share an office with that

7

man. I'd never get anything done just imagining how much satisfaction I'd get kicking him in the balls."

"So, kick him in the balls and get over it. We need this office." Mallory ran her hands over the walnut stained windowsill. "Where else are we going to find hard wood floors, a private restroom and kitchen, and in the old moneyed TCU neighborhood?"

For the first time since recognizing Logan, Savannah focused on the suite, inhaling the scents of paint, varnish, and sawdust. Venturing further inside, she turned, absorbing the ambiance. "Upscale. And if we land a couple contracts, possibly we can afford the rent." This office fit their criteria like someone had custom designed it for them.

She stopped in mid-turn, catching site of Logan's tall, stocky frame propped against the door.

Except him.

He focused his stare on Savannah. "We can tear up the lease if this makes you uncomfortable."

Oh, wouldn't his ego love for her to admit that working with him would upset her?

"Why would I be uncomfortable?" she asked, staring into his navy blue eyes without flinching. "The suite's incredible."

Mallory turned to Savannah like she wasn't sure who'd spoken.

Partners By Design

Savannah caught the slight crease in Logan's forehead.

"Fine. The building opens next Monday. You two take this office. I'll use the smaller one. We can start moving in Saturday." He turned and strolled out of the suite as if she meant no more to him than last year's fads.

The tape measure scraped as Mallory let it rewind with a snap. "You're sure you want to do this?"

Logan was the one who'd first introduced Savannah to the charm of TCU and the distinctive old homes that surrounded it. She shrugged. "Our first priority is getting our business up and running, not to mention moving it out of our living room. Seeing Logan after all this time just caught me off guard."

"So you're over him?"

"Nothing to get over."

* * *

Of all the women and all the offices...

Savannah Holt.

Logan straddled the barstool next to Ross and gritted his teeth. Savannah had 'Caution: Emotional Suicide' stamped across her cute little ass in bold black letters.

Just seeing her had his stomach in knots.

He ordered a Heineken and watched the Dallas Cowboy Cheerleaders dance across the big screen as pool balls clicked and sunk into leather pockets on the far side of the room.

He couldn't afford for anything to interfere with his business right now. He needed to line up contracts to replace the lost income when his internship ended in December.

"So, boss, you out to get laid?"

Logan swiveled at the sound of Ross' voice and tilted his head for a better look at the little redheaded waitress giving them the eye from across the room.

"Laid or plastered." Logan wrapped his fingers around the green bottle neck, ignoring the glass the bartender plopped down.

Ross raised an eyebrow. "In the seven months I've worked for you, I've never seen you plastered. Hell, this is what, the third time you've even agreed to grab a beer after work."

Logan took a long swig then nodded toward the pool tables. "Loser springs for dinner."

"Another Michelob draft." Ross exchanged conspiratorial grins with the bartender. "He's laboring under the delusion that he can beat me at pool. Juggling three jobs. I knew he'd crack."

The bartender drew a beer and placed it on the bar in front of Ross. "He sounds a little wired to me."

Logan grabbed his beer and made his way toward the tables. A little wired?

Major understatement. There were at least twenty things he should be doing tonight instead of hanging out in a bar, but after running into Savannah, he couldn't concentrate on any of them.

He sunk the three-ball on the break. "Solids."

A tight little butt in khaki shorts bumped against his hip. "Anybody ever tell you your ass looks good in denim?"

His gaze roamed over Marci's curves. "Not until now."

"Thought you forgot me." The redhead's hand grazed his ass as she glanced at his half full beer bottle. "Ready for another one?"

"Maybe later," Logan said.

She flashed a dimple and sauntered away balancing a tray of empty bottles on one hand and wiggling her fingers at him over her shoulder with the other.

Logan banked the seven-ball into the side pocket and lined up a shot on the two. "Wings sound good for dinner?"

Ross nodded and cocked his head for a better view as Marci nudged her way to the counter to place an order. "She's a fox."

The two-ball dropped into the pocket. "She's okay."

"Wake up, dude. I'm in here three or four nights a week and she never grabs my ass."

Marci had the skills to relieve one type pressure. At least she had helped a month ago, but going home with Marci tonight wouldn't solve his problem with Savannah.

After losing three games, Ross propped his cue back in the rack. "When did you ever take enough time off work to learn to play pool?"

"The first couple years in college, I hustled pool for meals." Logan handed his cue to the guy waiting for their table.

"So even sports are a job to you." Ross sighed. "Spicy wings okay?"

"Works for me."

Ross dropped into a chair. "You need to learn to chill."

"Can't until after December. I teach the night class to pay for my Masters. I landed the paid internship by agreeing to manage the construction projects for the guy. I've got to have my business set up and some clients by the time I graduate or I'll starve."

Marci placed a bowl of peanuts on the table. "Two more beers, guys?"

"Thanks. And an order of the flaming hot jalapeno wings." Ross gave Marci the once over as she headed back toward the bar. "If you're not interested in her, you don't mind if I take a shot?"

"Go for it." Logan grabbed a handful of peanuts. With twenty-five hours of work to cram into every twenty-four hour day, he'd been operating on four or five hours sleep a night. These days he got more excited over a good night's sleep than sex. How pathetic was that?

"My shift's over at midnight." Marci plunked an ice-cold beer on the table and cocked a brow at Logan.

He offered her a smile, but shook his head. "Maybe another night. I'm done in."

After a half a dozen hot wings, Logan left Ross flirting with Marci and crawled into his truck. He rested his forehead against the steering wheel and groaned. Facing Savannah today had brought it all back. High school romance or not, she'd had him wrapped from the instant they'd met.

Every detail of their short relationship was scorched into his brain. Savannah had been wild and free and spontaneous. A lifetime ago and he still remembered the sticky taste of her strawberry flavored lip-gloss. The couple inches of exposed belly between her sexy little shirt and shorts. The way her lips parted just before he kissed her. The agony in her eyes the night he'd broken up with her.

What was he supposed to say if she brought up the past? He was no more man enough to open Pandora's damn box now than he'd been at eighteen.

Partners By Design

Chapter Two

The power of live theater enthralled Savannah. She accepted her date's hand and pulled herself to her feet as the final bars of Phantom of the Opera ended and the cast took their bows. The Phantom, Christine, and Raoul would be acting out their roles in her fantasies for days.

Oh for the simplicity of summer afternoons spent at the theater with her mother and sister. Mom bought them new dresses to attend performances of Cinderella or The Sound of Music.

Tom cupped her elbow and led her through the crowd and into the packed Bass Performance Hall lobby. She waited as he stopped to chat with half the people they passed.

Savannah smiled as he introduced her to an older couple. The gentleman's royal blue shirt coordinated perfectly with his wife's sequined gown. As they rambled on about their recent anniversary trip to Europe, Savannah marveled how a couple seemed so happy after forty years of marriage.

"So, how long have you been dating our Tom?" The woman pulled Savannah aside from the men. "Such a nice young man. He and our daughter, Mathilda, were like brother and sister as kids. His parents are delightful."

Savannah shrugged. "First date." Would it be rude to mention her interior design business? She wasn't sure of the proper etiquette in this situation, but she had to get some contracts in the works. The sooner their business took off, the sooner they could afford a different office.

An office away from Logan Reid.

The gentleman clasped Tom on the shoulder. "When you see your father, remind him he still owes me a round of golf."

"He's afraid he'll have to buy you another bottle of scotch, as bad as he lost last time." Tom shook the man's hand and moved on to a group of four other men.

Savannah studied Tom as he worked the crowd. The consummate, successful businessman. He had the looks, the style, and the charm to make everyone love him. Rungs above Logan in every aspect and not just for his dark wavy hair, tailor made suit, and Italian shoes. Tom Truesdale had the mark of a gentleman.

Mom had labeled him excellent husband potential. Except Savannah couldn't imagine rolling over every morning with him on the pillow next to her. He probably slept in a tie.

After a half hour of schmoozing, the crowd dwindled. Tom slipped his arm around her waist and headed to the curb to wait for the limo.

"You know everyone in this town."

"The important ones at least." He straightened her diamond drop necklace, brushing his fingers against her throat. "You're very quiet."

"Wondering if it would be too pushy to put in a good word for my business. Not that I want to exploit your friends, but, I mean, if anyone happens to require an interior designer..." Well, that sounded desperate. She *was* desperate.

"Consider it done." He took her hand. "Your mother mentioned you're laboring under a slight financial strain."

She cringed. Slight strain? Dire straits was closer to the truth. Savannah shook her head. "My partner and I have it under control."

"There are vacancies in our building where you could hang out your shingle."

"Thanks, but we rented an office today." She gritted her teeth behind her smile. Her financial security had gone into the grave with her dad. Since his death, she'd watched her mother go from not having a care in the world beyond being a good wife and mother to living in fear of losing everything. Over the past six years, Mom had hopped from one bad relationship to another until she'd let Donald move in last Christmas. He wasn't a bad guy. The problem was that he hadn't had as much money as he'd let on to Mom and she'd sunk further into debt.

Partners By Design

Relying on men hadn't worked well for Mom and Savannah wasn't anywhere near as poised or beautiful as her mother. The last thing she needed was a rich guy trying to take care of her. The only insurance policy against financial desperation, now and for the future, was to make her business pay off.

"I thought a late dinner might be nice."

Savannah fanned her neck with the Playbill. It must be at least ninety tonight. Not a breeze stirring. Her panty hose and black dress clung to her heated skin and all she wanted was to go home, strip off these clothes, and step into a cool shower.

"The play was wonderful, Tom. But it's been a long day. Not very hungry and I have an early morning tomorrow."

He frowned, but instructed the driver toward the little house Savannah and Mallory shared. "I'd love to see you again."

"Tonight was nice, but I'm so buried in my business, I really don't have the time for anything else right now."

Tom's gaze never left hers. "Appreciate the honesty. But I think you should give me more of a chance than one date."

Her chest tightened. At a young age Savannah had learned not to trust men. Not that she enjoyed feeling that way, it was her survival instinct. Their words meant nothing, zero, zip, nada. Empty syllables.

Partners By Design

Logan had been the first to make promises then desert her, but he hadn't been the last. "Maybe down the road when things settle in. You'd be wasting your time with me right now."

* * *

Saturday morning couldn't have come fast enough for Savannah.

"We have arrived!" She sang and danced an energetic mini-cheer routine to the tune of I Will Survive.

"We're moving in, partner!" Mallory high-fived her and bounced from one Puma sneaker to the other while Savannah inserted the shiny gold key into the door. At least there was no sign of Logan.

Not that it mattered.

No reason he should bother her. The last time she'd dealt with him, she'd been a naïve, hormonal teenager. Now she was a mature woman who made decisions based on knowledge and common sense, not her libido.

She lugged a box of computer components and wires upstairs into their office, and wiped beads of sweat off her forehead. The landlord hadn't turned on the air conditioner. But who'd expect to need it the first weekend in October? "I'll open the windows."

Mallory deposited a plastic bin of supplies in the corner and spread her arms to embrace the office in a giant bear hug. "I'll run get another load."

"Wait and I'll help you haul the desk

Partners By Design

in." Savannah followed her friend through the main lobby, basking in anticipation of opening their doors in the TCU neighborhood.

As they headed out, Savannah opened the door for a couple of other box-toting women. They nodded toward the giant moving van at the curb and explained they worked for the real estate firm which occupied the entire east side of the first floor.

Mallory crawled inside the van and positioned herself behind the desk. Savannah tugged from the outside, struggling to move the heavy cherry wood furniture. It had been a tight fit going in and had shifted in transit.

Savannah glanced at the team of men unloading furniture out of the truck for the real estate office. She wiped her forehead and tugged on the desk legs, backing into a solid chest.

"Here, let me grab that." An arm snaked around her to take the desk.

Logan! Electric currents shot through her veins and her knees threatened to buckle. Every nerve responded to his clean, masculine scent, to the feel of his nearness.

Don't react, Savannah. Remember-Beneath that sensual aura beats the heart of a cold-hearted jerk. Oh, he had the act down. Charm a girl with his low key, boy-next-door, sweet and harmless appearance. Begin with a few nights of intense make-out sessions and ease into mind-blowing sex. Then on to the next conquest.

Partners By Design

"We've got it."

Logan dropped his hand and stepped to the side.

Good. Mallory shoved and Savannah yanked with double determination, but the desk didn't budge.

Wordlessly, Logan quirked his head to one side and pointed toward the wedged desk.

She moved aside and watched as he tapped the side of the wood with his palm. Mallory shoved and it slid into his arms as if he'd said 'Come to Daddy.'

Fickle desk was obviously female.

Savannah draped the blanket on the metal dolly and held it in place while Logan maneuvered the desk into position.

He hadn't shaved this morning and the dark shadow made him look older. Not movie star handsome. Not classic dark good looks like her date last night. Not even the classic face that turned every woman's head. Just down-to-Earth, hard-working masculinity.

Her body temperature rose with each flexed muscle.

Mallory bounded out of the van and clasped Logan's shoulder. "Great timing."

He returned her grin and pushed the dolly down the sidewalk toward the front door.

Savannah's heart skipped at his once-familiar smile, but she shook it off, or tried to. The last thing she needed in her

20

stressful life was another disastrous relationship.

'Good' and 'man' shouldn't be allowed in the same sentence. Her ex-boyfriend had seemed perfect. Safe. Predictable. He scheduled every minute on his phone calendar. She frowned. Including sex. Why bother?

Nothing about her short relationship with Logan had been organized, or planned, or controllable.

Mallory leaned over and whispered in Savannah's ear. "At least he's useful."

"And smug." Savannah hoisted another box and locked the van.

"Stick to your plan. Ignore him. Let me deal with Mr. Reid." Mallory darted ahead to hold the door.

Since Wednesday, Mal had hounded Savannah to fill her in regarding Logan. And no matter how hard Savannah fought to forget, snippets of memories popped into her mind. Like strip driving the night he'd taught her to drive a stick shift. Her first hot glimpse of his chest when he'd lost his shirt. The intensity of their first make-out session.

<u>You and Me Against the World</u> chimed from her purse. Savannah dropped the box in her new office with a thud and dug her ringing cell phone out as she watched Logan position the desk.

Mom was out of bed before ten AM? Savannah pressed the phone to her ear. "Good morning, Mom."

Partners By Design

"Donald moved out," Mom wailed. "Dumped me for some anorexic socialite who hasn't seen the high side of twenty. You'd have thought the heartless jerk might've at least transferred the money to cover my house payment. And now I discover he didn't pay last month's either. How did I pick the only guy at the country club as poor as me? He could have been honest. Where am I supposed to come up with thirty-eight-hundred dollars by the fifteenth?"

Savannah squeezed her eyes shut. The relationship with Donald-don't-call-me-Don had lasted ten months. That was two months longer than Mom's previous relationship.

As she listened to the latest mama drama, Savannah turned her back on Logan.

"After all I put into that relationship." Mom let out an exasperated sigh and adopted her more cajoling southern tone. "Sweetie, how about Bridgette Truesdale's son you went out with last night?"

"Over."

"After one date?"

"I don't have time for a relationship, Mom."

"The right man could be significantly more lucrative than a business. I don't understand you sometimes. What are you thinking?"

Savannah gnashed her teeth. "For starters, how to be self-sufficient and support myself."

"Savannah, I've maintained our membership at the country club to give you the venue to meet the right people. Find the right man."

Hmmm. Possibly part of Mom's relationship issues stemmed from basing her choices on financial potential?

Constance Holt let out a breath. "Honey, I know I promised not to ask for money, but I could lose our home, the home Daddy bought for us."

Savannah squeezed the phone and fought to keep tension out of her voice. She was struggling to make her own bills. "We'll talk tonight."

Savannah clicked the phone shut and jumped as Logan leaned over her shoulder. "Mommy Dearest still yanking your chain?"

"What does that mean?" she snapped. "You hardly knew my mother."

He hesitated and cocked an eyebrow. "Sorry." He grabbed the other end of the desk and helped Mallory move it back to the original position. "That good?"

"Yep." Mallory flashed an impish grin.

"Cool. Yell if you need help. I've got a truck full of boxes to unload." He gave Savannah a cursory nod and headed out the door.

Savannah tried not to stare at the way the tight, faded denim hugged his butt.

"Great ass." Mallory sighed.

Partners By Design

Savannah pointed her cell phone at Mallory. "Stuff it."

Mallory's grin spread ear to ear. "What? What'd I say?"

By lunchtime, Mallory and Savannah had unloaded the van and were ready for the next load.

Savannah pushed the front door to the office building open and almost knocked Quentin, Mallory's boyfriend, down.

"Whoa." He steadied himself, and then reached past her to drape Mallory over one arm and plant a dramatic kiss on her lips. "How's the move coming?"

Mallory straightened and narrowed her eyes at the black Porsche parked at the end of the sidewalk. "The idea was to bring your truck, Einstein."

"Dad's transmission went out so he had to use mine to haul Mom's horse to Tucson for the competition." With curly red hair and freckles, Quentin had the kind of face that made people smile. He grinned at Savannah. "We can get by with your van, right?"

Mallory pushed him away. "You haven't seen all we have to move."

"I can make a run in the truck, if it'll help," Logan offered, coming up from behind.

Quentin extended his hand. "You must be Logan. I'm Quentin, Mallory's, uh, hmmm."

"Boyfriend." Mallory gave him a good-natured shove and beamed at Logan. "That'd be great."

Savannah had no intention of cramming into that pickup against Logan. She kept her expression neutral. "The three of you run on and I'll track down some sandwiches while you're gone."

Logan shot her a look that said he knew she was avoiding him. Or maybe it was her imagination. Either way, she turned and headed back inside the office.

★ ★ ★

Sunday morning a week later Logan arrived at the office hoping for peace and quiet only to find Savannah at the small reception desk. Why couldn't she work in her own office? Both phone lines rang on all the phones, so there was no reason for her to work out here except to torment him.

How was he supposed to handle seeing her every day? Keep it casual. Whatever happened, he couldn't let her get to him. Couldn't risk her learning the truth.

"Good morning," he offered, shifting the box of *Architect Digest* to the other arm.

She slid a stack of blank paper into a drawer without looking up. "Good morning." She wore the same frigid, void of emotion expression he'd seen yesterday, and the day before yesterday, and the day before that.

Screw it. He lugged the box into his office. He wasn't sure if she honest to

Partners By Design

God hated him or was just determined to appear that way. But, why shouldn't she hate him?

He thought back to the spontaneous, fiery-tempered girl with the aquamarine eyes. She'd been exciting and unpredictable. Nothing had stopped Savannah in those days. By the time he'd known her twenty-four hours, he'd been down for the count. Hours? Hell, by the time he'd known her twenty-four minutes.

But even if she were interested, the possibility of starting back up was a powder keg waiting for a match.

For his good and Savannah's, he needed to maintain a distance. He pushed Savannah Holt to the back of his mind and unpacked the box. Where was Mallory? He could be around her without feeling like a slimy rodent.

Her boyfriend seemed cool too, even if he did drive a sixty-thousand dollar Porsche. Must be more money in thoroughbred horses than he'd figured. Yet how much of a snob could the guy be with horse dung on his boots?

He glanced at the display on his ringing cell phone. Great. "Hey, Kat. No, I can't make it for lunch and no, I haven't mentioned it." He held the phone away from his ear. "I said I would." Eventually.

"I'm in the market to hire someone. You said you and your friends needed to drum up business. They should make me a good deal, right?" Kat said.

Friends? She made it sound as if they were in business together. "You can't let us get settled in first?" Logan dropped a handful of magazines back into the box.

"Nathan finally agreed to spend the money and I'm not about to give him time to change his mind."

"You're not going to let this go, are you?" Hoping to stay out of the middle, he walked back into the reception area. "Hold on."

He put his hand over the phone and addressed Savannah. "My sister found out my suitemates are interior designers and wants to know if you'd be interested in taking a look at her master bedroom. Shouldn't be much of a job. It's about nine by nine."

Savannah's head came up, but so did her eyebrow. Did she think he was creating business as a come on? He put the phone back to his ear. "Hey. I'll let you talk to Savannah." He shoved the phone into her hand and went back into his office.

A couple minutes later, Savannah appeared in the doorway and placed his phone on the sofa. "Kathy suggested I ride out to their place with you this afternoon to take a look. I'll follow in my car. Don't want to interfere with your plans."

He should have known he'd get pulled in, but the sooner he introduced them, the sooner he could bow out. "Taking two vehicles is crazy. It's an hour drive." Unless she'd changed, Savannah was the world's worst at following directions.

Partners By Design

She'd end up in Oklahoma before she realized she was lost. "I'll drive. It'll give me an excuse not to stay long anyway."

Her jaw jutted out. "Fine."

Had Kat mentioned where she lived? "You sure about this?"

Savannah shot him one of those icy, detached looks. What the hell had happened to the vivacious girl he'd fallen in love with? The girl with a mischievous grin lurking just beneath the surface. "About what? You don't want me working for your sister?"

Her snippy attitude needed an adjustment. "Eagle Mountain Lake spark any alarms with you?"

She looked up, expression blank. "Should it?"

"Kat bought my grandmother's lake house."

Color drained from Savannah's face down to her pink glossed toenails.

Partners By Design

Chapter Three

As Logan pulled up to the house, Savannah focused on the road-stripe yellow Mustang parked in the drive. Anything to avoid looking at that house.

For the entire ride she'd typed aimlessly on her laptop, trying to focus on the money this contract could bring in and not their destination.

Coming here was important to her career. Showing Logan that coming here didn't affect her was important to her self-esteem.

Before he had time to make it around to open her door, she slid down from the truck. The place looked exactly like she remembered it. "Such a great house."

"Yeah. Spent some of the best times of my adolescence here," he said.

She shouldered her purse and forced herself not to flinch.

The front door opened and a woman stepped out and embraced Logan in a bear hug. "Long time no see."

He stood back and motioned Savannah forward. "Savannah Holt, my sister, Kathy Barnaby."

If Savannah's name struck a chord,

Kathy didn't let on. After all, they'd met only once. And that was a long time ago.

Savannah stopped inside the door. At least she and Logan weren't alone. She placed her satchel beside the Caribbean blue couch and wiped her palms on her slacks.

With any luck, Kathy would show her to the room she wanted to redecorate and they could negotiate a contract. Then Savannah could get the hell out of here.

"Hey, Bro," a young guy said from his sprawled position on the sofa. "Decide to grace us with your presence?"

"Savannah, my kid brother, Dale." Logan narrowed one eye at him. "How's college?"

"What? You think I can't cut it?" Dale draped one leg over the sofa arm and dangled a glowing white sneaker.

Savannah ignored the exchange. The touchy attitude trait seemed to run in the male species of the Reid family.

"Just making conversation." Logan turned and headed across the room toward the kitchen.

Savannah followed Kathy and the mouth-watering aroma of spicy spaghetti sauce. "Nathan, meet the woman who's going to turn our tiny bedroom into a romantic retreat."

Nathan returned Logan's handshake and grinned at Savannah. "As long as it's cheap. I'll settle for being able to get to the closet without climbing over the bed."

"I'm sure we can come up with a workable solution." Savannah grinned, noticing that whoever had redone the kitchen hadn't spared any cost. Top of the line stainless appliances and gray granite countertops.

"Lunch will be ready in fifteen minutes," Nathan said.

Savannah gulped. Lunch?

Nathan filled two glasses with ice and nodded at Logan. "You in on this too?"

"I only drove out because Kat mentioned you were cooking." Logan lifted the lid and inhaled the scent of bubbling sauce.

"So have you seen the folks lately?" Kathy asked, almost challenged.

"I saw Mom last week," Logan said, reaching for the glass of iced tea Nathan pushed his way. He fished the sprig of mint out and dropped it in the trash before taking a drink.

"But not Dad?" Kathy persisted, handing Savannah a matching glass.

Logan's jaw tensed. "We manage Thanksgiving and Christmas without throwing punches. Be happy."

Dale trudged into the kitchen. "Yeah, 'cause we all know what a party holidays with the family turn into." He grabbed a soda from the fridge and disappeared out the back door.

Savannah twisted her hands and looked

out the window, uncomfortable in the center of the family squabble.

Reaching around her, Logan snatched a slice of raw carrot from the salad. As his chest brushed against her, he put a steadying hand on her arm.

She rolled her shoulder and slid out of range. The last thing she needed was his touch. Not here. Not now. Not ever.

He moved to the other side of the bar and leaned against the cabinet, taking a drink.

Savannah felt him watching, waiting for her to freak out. She gripped the barstool, then dropped her hands, only to grip it again. She hated being on his turf, with his family. In this house.

Nathan raked uniform tomato wedges off a cutting board into the salad. "Logan only shows up for the food, but we don't hold that it against him."

"I cook." Logan took another swig.

Kathy nudged Savannah. "Anything that comes out of a box and goes straight into the microwave doesn't qualify."

Logan exchanged looks with Nathan. "This coming from the woman who married a professional chef because she couldn't stomach her own cooking. At least I know how to operate a grill."

"Great, you're helping with dinner tonight," Nathan said.

"We're not staying for dinner!" Savannah blurted out. Her cheeks grew hot and she forced a grin. "Sorry, I mean I have other plans." She didn't, but she wasn't about to endure anymore of this house than necessary.

Logan tightened his grip on the glass and walked out the back door.

* * *

After a lunch of listening to his kid brother bait Logan, Savannah watched Dale and Nathan race away from the dock on Jet Skis. Dale was looking for attention and she was amazed Logan hadn't jumped across the table and strangled him.

"Ready to take a look?" Kathy asked her.

Exhibiting little expression, Logan shoved the placemats aside on the kitchen table then opened a folder.

Savannah just wanted to get this over with and get out of this house before she self-combusted. Being here added salt to old wounds, but enduring Logan watching her for the slightest reaction ripped them open and ground it in.

She followed Kathy down the short hallway, focusing straight ahead as they passed the guest bedroom. No way was she even looking in there today or she'd lose what little control she had left.

"This is our room." Kathy waved her hand indicating the master suite. "Similar size and ambiance of a broom closet. Not looking for miracles, but anything to lighten it up and give us more space would be fantastic."

Partners By Design

Focusing, Savannah fished her tape measure out and jotted the room size down on her notepad. "I'd get rid of those heavy drapes and sheers. Install a blind that fits inside the window encasement and lets in the natural sunlight. There are some great styles on the market."

Kathy nodded. "Light would be good."

"Replacing the window with French doors and adding a deck would extend your space. You could even knock out a wall and enlarge the room, but that requires an architect." Savannah gulped, realizing her blunder.

Kathy followed the direction of her eyes. "Sounds fantastic, but Nathan isn't willing to spend that kind of money."

"What's under this carpet?" Savannah asked, letting out a relieved breath. "A wood floor or even a laminate would give it a more updated look. Are you attached to the wainscoting?" Genuine pine or not, it made the room seem half again as small.

"I hate it."

The roar of Jet Skis echoed through the open windows as Nathan and Dale coasted alongside the dock.

"Guys are back. Anything else you need to look at in here?"

Savannah shook her head and Kathy led the way out of the bedroom.

Nathan burst through the back door, grabbed a towel off the stack, and scrubbed the dripping water off his dark hair. "Who's next? The water's like glass.

Partners By Design

Might be the last chance before it gets cold." He eyed Savannah.

She stretched to see out as two young girls roared past on a purple Jet Ski. Dale revved the engine and raced after them. "I've never been on a Jet Ski. I'd wreck it."

"Logan can take you for a spin," Kathy suggested.

"No!" Savannah swallowed hard and took a deep breath. "I... I didn't bring a swimsuit."

"I have one you can borrow," Kathy offered. "I mean, you were nice enough to drive all the way out to the lake."

Logan snapped his pencil into two pieces. "I've got swim trunks in the pickup." He cocked an eyebrow. "Unless you're afraid of water."

Her blood boiled and she clenched her fist to keep from slapping that smug look off his face. So this was how he wanted to play it? He was pushing, challenging her to admit that getting on a Jet Ski with him bothered her?

"Why not?" She flashed Logan a killer smile.

* * *

Nathan met Logan halfway to the lake and gave him a good-natured shove, nodding toward Savannah dangling her feet off their private dock. "Talk about a nice swerve. Wait until you get a load of that bikini."

Partners By Design

"She and I are not together. Never happen."

"Something's happening. The electricity between you two could power my house for a month."

Logan flashed a glare capable of shutting down his construction workers in mid taunt.

Nathan nodded. "Got it. You're more into short, pudgy, maybe a wart on her nose. And who wants personality?"

"Screw you."

As Nathan continued toward the house, his laughter followed Logan.

At least Nathan didn't know Savannah had been the first--the only--woman to ever get to him. But the wall between them stood as insurmountable today as it had the night eight years ago when he'd ended the relationship. No way could he ever explain why he'd walked away. That wild, spontaneous sixteen-year-old girl he'd fallen in love with would never have believed him. The rigid twenty-four year old woman sitting on the weathered dock wouldn't handle the truth any better.

His mouth went dry at Savannah's graceful sway as she stood. Indecent didn't come close to describing the red bikini. And her legs never stopped.

He finger-combed his sweaty hair from his forehead. The air wasn't moving today. Getting wet might actually be good.

Savannah backed away from the edge and turned. His gaze skimmed her shoulders

Partners By Design

and landed on the tiny mole above her left breast. His tongue touched his top lip and he tried to erase the image of kissing her there. The thrill of two kids experimenting with their first sexual encounter.

    God, he was so sunk.

Chapter Four

Logan flinched as Savannah rubbed her hands up and down her arms. Attempting to scrub away his touch? Evidently she didn't have the same fond memories of their time together as he did.

Screw it. He scooted forward on the Jet Ski, and motioned to the padded seat behind him.

The boat rocked as Savannah straddled the seat and placed one hand on either side of his foam life jacket. "We hit rough water you're going for a swim if you don't hold on tighter," he yelled over the engine.

She inched a little closer and clasped her hands across his stomach, but she only touched the foam and not his skin.

Closing his eyes, he gripped the handlebars. What the hell had he been thinking when he'd goaded her into this?

As he pushed away from the dock and idled toward open water, he willed his body to relax. The engine vibrated, but the ride was tame enough as they coasted past the no wake buoy. He swung to the right and twisted the gas.

Savannah closed a death grip on his

waist.

He couldn't decide if he was having trouble breathing because of the wind hitting him in the face at forty miles per hour or Savannah plastered tight against his back.

I can do this. Just one quick tour around the lake.

Logan leaned to the left, eased into a wide turn, and yelled over his shoulder. "Lean with me."

As soon as the boat leveled out, she tried to scoot back, but the angle of the seat kept her pelvis snug against his butt. He wasn't comfortable with their position. The jolt from her legs pressed against his didn't even rank compared to the piercing lightning bolt when her body bumped his hip.

Don't think about it. Drive. Concentrate on the lake house architecture. Count the damn ducks. Anything except Savannah's bare legs bracketing his.

A hodgepodge of homes flanked the shore, ranging from sprawling ranch to modern glass masterpieces. If Kat drummed up some leads out here it could mean a sizeable boost to his business.

Savannah pointed at a small country blue bungalow bordered by a kaleidoscope of bright flowers. "Look how homey and inviting."

He cruised past a dilapidated rock house with an overgrown yard and

Partners By Design

ramshackle boathouse. "I'd like to get my hands on that one. Restore it to its original condition. Add a rock patio, a cover, an outside kitchen and ceiling fans."

"Nice," she said, getting into the mood.

"Hang on."

The Jet Ski lurched and she clutched his waist. Splinters of water stung his legs, but wild exhilaration exploded as they skimmed across the glassy surface like a high-speed motorcycle.

Or Savannah's little red Miata convertible sailing down a country road after a spring rain. Moon filtering through translucent clouds, cool wind in their faces, and heater warming their feet like a furnace on a cold winter night.

He tensed as she leaned her cheek against his life jacket. For the first time he didn't sense any hostility. And he wasn't sure if it made him happy or scared him senseless.

"Wait until you see the houses on the far side of the lake." He swung the Jet Ski around. They were more modern, and twice as large as those in Kat's neighborhood. He slowed as they approached and the small craft bobbed over the waves.

"Look at that one," she yelled over the engine. "The entire back of the house is glass." She pointed just as they hit a choppy wake from a passing ski boat. With only one hand holding on, she bounced backward off the seat and landed headfirst

Partners By Design

in the water.

Logan dove off the Jet Ski as she popped to the surface like a cork, coughing and choking.

"Can you breathe?" He grabbed around her waist. "Relax, I've got you."

She coughed out a mouthful of lake water and sucked air into her lungs.

He smoothed the hair from her face. "I should have warned you about that wake."

"It was my fault for not holding on." She tried to laugh and push away, but their bodies clung together like opposite magnetic poles.

How could the attraction remain so strong after so many years? Aquamarine eyes sparkled between wet, spiky lashes. The so kissable mouth he still tasted in his dreams, or nightmares.

He tightened his arms and pulled her against his chest. Her eyes drew him in. *I shouldn't do this.* Her moist lips parted only millimeters from his. *I'm playing with fire.* He cupped her face and watched her tongue moisten her lips.

When she placed her hand on his shoulder, he expected her to push away, but her fingers curled into his skin.

He grabbed her hand and kissed her palm then placed it behind his neck. So warm. Just one taste. His mouth moved to hers and as her eyes closed, he followed suit.

Her lips parted beneath his and he slid his tongue inside, reuniting his senses with Savannah. His emotions returned to that stormy spring night and the seductive, innocent girl he'd rescued from where she'd spun out in the jammed intersection.

Their hips bumped and a quick rush of fire shot through him as she free-floated in his arms. He kept his eyes closed, not wanting to break the spell. She wove her fingers in his hair and tugged him closer. All he could think about were her hands on his skin and her lips moving with his.

He cupped the back of her head, slid his other hand beneath the lifejacket, and pressed the small of her back.

He wanted to touch her all over. Explore how she'd changed. Mouth to mouth. Skin to skin. Breast to chest. And farther south. She ran her hands over his arms, and he almost lost it. Still not enough to squelch his curiosity, but he let Savannah maintain the lead.

Her fingers plunged beneath his lifejacket and walked up his chest. Still, he didn't open his eyes.

She gripped his waist and moved in closer. Her hot lips opened over his. Logan sucked her breath into his mouth and reacquainted himself with the essence of Savannah.

The front of his swim trunks pressed against her bikini. A jolt of electricity from the intimate contact took him back to the dock where they'd played and made out

Partners By Design

in the water a lifetime ago, or was it yesterday?

Savannah wrenched her mouth from his and shoved hard. "Stop!"

His mind struggled to catch up. He opened his eyes in time to see her swim for the Jet Ski, grab the back, and search for a foothold to pull herself up. As she scrambled onboard, he fell under the trance of her clumsy, indecent ascent.

By the time he tore his eyes away from her skimpy spandex clad derriere and her intention registered, it was too late. He swam hard toward the Jet Ski as the engine roared to life. "Savannah!"

With a quick glance over her shoulder, she twisted the handle and the ski lurched to the right. She straightened the handlebar and it careened across the water leaving him floating in her wake.

"Dammit!" He was at least a mile from Kat's. Granted, he could have used a little restraint, but she wasn't exactly resistant. "Dammit!"

He focused across the lake and paced his strokes. If somebody didn't pick him up or run him over, he might get back to Kat's in time for dinner. He should have guessed Savannah would take off. After all, not knowing how to drive a stick shift hadn't stopped her from tearing out in her brand new Miata the night they'd met.

She was amazing, always had been. On her sixteenth birthday, she'd caught her boyfriend making out with her best friend and stolen both their clothes. Hell, she'd even bought Logan dinner with money from the guy's wallet. He chuckled at the memory. She'd drawn him in so tight, his mind and body had thought of nothing else for days.

A roar in the distance caught his attention and he squinted, trying to determine if it was Savannah or some other boat. It was moving full out. And headed straight for him. He waved and pointed to the side, but she kept coming, closer and closer.

He kicked his feet to try to escape and yelled for her to turn. She didn't alter her path. Was she trying to run him over?

"Where is the brake?" she yelled as she flew by, missing him by no more than a foot.

She twisted the gas back and eased around. As she approached a second time, she allowed a good ten feet between them.

"Turn off the key!"

Killing the engine, she floated by.

"You trying to kill me or did you just come back to steal my pants?"

"Sorry." She wrinkled her nose and a dimple creased her right cheek. "I didn't know how to get back to the house."

"And here I thought you came back out of the goodness of your heart." Logan hoisted himself up behind her before she decided to take off again. "Since you're so good at this, you drive."

Partners By Design

He moved close, straddling her, and leaned in. "Just take it slow."

If she felt his erection against her bottom, she'd kick him off and never look back. He scooted back, putting a little distance between them.

She gave the gas a twist and Logan pointed across the lake. "Head for the Texas Flag." He rested one hand on her thigh and drawled into her ear. "Nothing to it, darlin'."

The ski wobbled and he reached to grab the handlebar and keep them straight.

Wet droplets dripped from her hair and ran down her arms as the wind left chill bumps in their path. Even doused in lake water, the familiar scent of her shampoo drew him in. The temptation to wrap his arms around her and warm them both almost took hold. He'd thought he could just move on with his life and forget Savannah Holt. Maybe if he'd never seen her again...

But she was even more off limits now than she'd been before. If they got involved, the truth would come out. And she'd be devastated. If he leveled with her now, would she ever be able to forgive him enough for them to make another try?

As they approached the dock, she turned the controls loose and let him guide the Jet Ski in. His arms caged her, forcing her to lean forward.

The position gave his body erotic ideas much more interesting than docking a damn boat.

Partners By Design

As soon as he looped the rope over the hook, she scurried onto the platform and headed up the wooden dock.

"Hey, slick. Lifejacket stays down here."

"Jerk!" Glaring, she stripped off the lifejacket and slung it at his head, then darted for the house.

He laughed, snagging the vest before it landed in the lake.

What had she been thinking? A fun, innocent jaunt around the lake? Yeah. Wearing a red string-bikini and wrapped around the first guy she'd ever had sex with.

The only guy in her entire twenty-four years who'd ever brought her to ecstasy. A guy whose kiss charged through her veins scorching a trail from her lips to her toes.

Stupid, stupid, stupid.

She grabbed a towel by the door and made a beeline toward the master bedroom, anxious to be in her own clothes before Logan finished securing the boat.

"Nathan's showering," Kathy said as she passed her in the hallway. "I moved your clothes to the spare bedroom."

No! Savannah froze. *I can't go in that room.* Or even think of undressing in there. A lump the size of a basketball lodged in her chest.

Kathy stared at her like she'd lost

her last marble. Did she know? Could she tell where Logan's hands and mouth had touched Savannah's body? Just like Mom had known the night Savannah had come home hours past curfew after having sex the first time. With Logan. In this house. In that room.

She choked down the acid taste of dread and took a couple steps, but her legs wobbled. Holding her breath and closing her eyes, she took the last step inside and closed the bedroom door behind her.

Breathe. In and out. Once her lungs were working again, she opened her eyes and looked around. Nothing had changed. Same white Cape Cod curtains, same baby blue paint. Same--bed. She blinked at the image of her and Logan stretched out on the antique brass bed. Two kids, sweaty and on fire with passion, exploring the electrifying magic of the opposite sex for the first time. She swiped at her tears. At least it'd been <u>her</u> first time.

The quivering started with her legs and worked its way upward until her entire body trembled.

Don't think about it.

She remembered how Logan felt on top of her, inside her. Her body flamed to the memory. How he'd kissed and caressed. How he'd touched her so tenderly and not forced her. Cradled her until she'd slept in his arms.

Tears burned her eyes and streamed down her face.

Partners By Design

Just put on your clothes and get out of here.

She shucked off the revealing red scraps of fabric, stared in the mirror at her swollen lips, and swiped at her mascara-smudged raccoon eyes with the towel.

The musky scent of Logan's aftershave clung to his tee shirt and jeans, folded on the bed. She stroked the soft cotton then jerked her hand back. That night had been magical. A fantasy. But it hadn't meant the same to him.

Sixteen days! Sixteen damn days from the night she met Logan Reid until he'd shattered her life, her dreams, her innocence.

Her hands shook so bad she couldn't even button her blouse.

She wouldn't survive Logan again.

She had more sense than to let this happen. There were other men in this world. Men who hadn't broken her heart. Nice men. Safe ones.

Men like Tom Truesdale.

When Savannah came out, she almost ran into Logan. He stood in the hall, waiting to change. Careful to give him as much space as feasible, she backed against the doorframe as he entered the miniscule bedroom.

He leaned close, but didn't touch her. "It was just a kiss."

Her anger exploded. "You know damn

well that was not just a kiss!"

He gripped her arm, hauled her back into the bedroom, and shut the door.

She didn't wait to hear his excuses. "You've enjoyed this, haven't you? You've been watching me squirm like an amoeba under a microscope since the second we arrived."

Logan turned her loose, but he kept his stance in front of the door. "I warned you Kat lived in this house."

She darted to the other side of the room, putting the bed between them. "How many other virgins did you bring here?"

His expression softened. "Only you."

"Argh!" She glared. Those smooth lines were not going to work on her, not this time. "I'm not that gullible anymore." Giving vent to her temper, she swiped his clothes up and tossed them out the open window.

Logan held a finger to his lips. "Keep your voice down." He eased around the bed and reached a hand out. She glimpsed that teenage boy in his face, the uncertainty and sweetness. The innocence and adventure.

"Why, Logan? Why were we on a whirlwind skyrocket ride one night then-- nothing? No explanation. You just--left." She moved close. "I loved you!"

His eyes widened, he blinked, his mouth opened, then shut. She could see his brain spinning, but not a word. His face turned alabaster. Total, consuming fear.

Partners By Design

"We were young. I...It was intense," he stammered, taking a step back, away from her. His Adam's apple bobbed. "I'll just retrieve my jeans off the front lawn." He grabbed his shoes and bolted out of the room.

She dropped down on the bed, and then sprang back up as if it had thorns and backed against the wall. Mom had always said that he'd gotten what he wanted and lost interest. But if that was all there was why did he look so devastated?

Guilt? Embarrassment? Was there something else?

Logan's heart threatened to pound a hole in his chest. He'd had to find out if that spark was still burning in Savannah, but in reigniting her emotions, he'd unleashed feelings in himself he'd kept buried for eight years.

"Savannah's the one, isn't she?"

He looked up with a start and met his sister's dark blue eyes. He couldn't deal with this. Not now. "Kat, don't."

"She's the jailbait you and Daddy had it out over?"

Had it out over? Hell, his whole damn life had crashed and burned that night. He'd left home with a duffel bag jammed full of clothes and his worn out pickup and he'd been making his own way ever since. "I'm not talking about this."

He turned toward the front door and escape, but found Savannah standing in the hall, wide eyes staring straight through him.

Clenching his teeth, he fought to keep his voice from cracking as he pushed his way past her. "I'll be in the truck."

Logan grabbed his clothes off the lawn then hauled himself into the pickup cab and started the engine. He tugged his shirt over his head, as the air conditioner raised chill bumps on his sunburned arms. What the hell had he expected? He should have known what would happen if he brought her here.

Savannah opened the passenger door and dropped her satchel on the floorboard. "Can we talk about what happened back then--before?"

He jabbed his fingers through his damp hair. "Nothing to gain."

"I think I understand now." She buckled her seatbelt.

Understand? He pulled onto the street without looking at her. The events of that night were beyond even his comprehension. And he'd lived through it.

"You walked away because you were eighteen and I was sixteen. You were afraid of going down for statutory rape."

That was what she was keying in on? A thought that had not entered his mind until after the relationship was unequivocally over. He stopped at the intersection and closed his eyes. "Yeah, that was it."

"Logan, we were in high school. We

both wanted to. Nobody would have blamed you." She placed her hand on his cheek and forced him to face her. "Why didn't you call me?"

"Because..." He struggled for a plausible answer. Even if the threat of criminal charges had scared him off before, it was a non-issue now. The vision of her psycho tramp of a mother holding Savannah's pink cell phone came into focus. "Your cell phone was disconnected."

"My what--?" Her face cleared. "I lost it."

He turned forward in the seat. "Whatever."

She grabbed his arm and leaned in, staring into his eyes. "So it was that easy for you to forget me?"

Her pleading expression ripped at his insides, but if she didn't back off, things were going to get a million times worse. "Like you said, we were in high school. It was hormones."

Her eyes glistened. "And back there in the lake just now?"

Back off, Savannah. Don't make me destroy you. Who was he kidding thinking they could ever be friends? The only way they could work together and not get involved was if she continued to hate him.

Forcing himself to hold her stare, he raised one eyebrow. "What did you expect? It's always been lust with us."

But watching her flinch and cross her arms over her stomach, another chunk of him died. The pain in his heart was just as raw as that night years ago when he'd walked away the first time.

They could never be together. Her damn mother had made sure of that.

Out of desperation, he flipped the radio on and cranked the volume up to ear splitting rock, eliminating further conversation.

Partners By Design

Chapter Five

Not tonight! Savannah groaned at the sight of Mom's gold Cadillac parked in the drive. Hadn't she had enough frustration for one day? Was it asking too much to be left alone for one evening to get past this?

Logan's words cut deep. Savannah had always believed Mom had been right about Logan. She'd always said that after he'd gotten what he wanted, he'd moved on. He'd never had true feelings for Savannah.

Still, something niggled at her that there might be more, that he was hiding something. He'd confessed too fast, too easy. But what could it matter now? Her future required a more solid base than lust.

She set her shoulders and opened the door to deal with the next person on the agenda tonight. What did Mom need that couldn't wait until tomorrow? Oh yeah. Determining how to pay her bills without Donald-don't-call-me Don.

Mal met Savannah at the door and wrapped her in a hug. "You're okay. We've been worried sick."

"Worried?" Mallory had known where she was. Still, Mal could always be counted on to keep a secret. Even if there was no secret to keep. However, in this case it was probably best that she hadn't told Savannah's mother.

Mom looked her up and down. "What happened? You're a mess. Where've you been all afternoon?"

Savannah tugged at her stiff, lake-water-caked hair and told herself Mom's clipped tone was only concern. "Long story."

"You didn't answer your cell. I was ready to call out the militia."

Savannah eased past her and dropped her purse on the end table. "Since when do I have to ask permission to make plans?"

Mom stopped in her tracks.

Mallory took a step back.

"Sorry." Closing her eyes, Savannah squelched her temper. Not fair to take her frustration with Logan out on them. She took a seat on the sofa and forced a smile. "Did Mallory tell you we moved into the office?"

Mom dropped back down in the chair. "Yes, that's great. So why don't you look happy?"

Because I just allowed Logan Reid to kiss me senseless and seeing him every day will be my worst nightmare. She shrugged. "Just realizing that sharing an office may not be the most professional approach."

Mallory looked between Savannah and Mom and jumped to her feet. "For the

Partners By Design

record, I have no problem with it." She grabbed her purse and grinned. "Well then, I'll leave you two to your own plans. I'm meeting friends."

She closed the door behind her and Mom frowned. "Can we afford an office along with everything else?"

We? "Mom, if I don't get the business going, we can't afford anything."

"Fine, so you were working?" she said with a resigned sigh. "You couldn't answer your cell?"

Savannah resented having to justify her actions to her mother. If she didn't want to answer the phone, she didn't have to. Okay, so maybe she was just in a seriously bad mood tonight. "Left it in the truck."

Mom fingered a tangled strand of Savannah's hair. "Truck? Your new suite mate's truck?"

"I got a contract to decorate the master bedroom at a lake house on Eagle Mountain. If I can bring it in under budget, maybe even for the entire house. Everyone was riding Jet Skis and I took a tumble. You know me. If anyone's going to make a fool of herself..." And falling off a Jet Ski was nothing compared to the rest of the afternoon. She stood.

Mom grabbed her hand and squeezed. "You hop in the shower and I'll give Bridgette a call. Rush it up. They're expecting us for dinner at seven."

Bridgette Truesdale? "Dinner?

Tonight? It's six-twenty."

"I'll let them know we're running a little late."

"Tom's parents? Mom, I'm not dating Tom." Squeezing her eyes shut, Savannah tried to get a grip on the day. First, Logan and that stupid kiss had her off balance. Now this?

"Well, he knows we're coming for dinner and he had no issue with it."

Why couldn't she just love someone like Tom? It would be so easy. He was everything a woman needed, wanted. With Logan, there was no chance for a future. There never had been. And today, she'd finally gotten her answer. It was just lust.

Mom gave her a quick pat on the shoulder. "Now get a move on. Bridgette still wants you to give her ideas on redoing her formal living room."

Savannah groaned as she shut the bathroom door. Sometimes she wondered whether she and her mother were even related. Mom evaluated men by their occupation, bank account, appearance, clothes. And if they didn't have a membership in the country club, well, why bother?

* * *

Savannah sat across the Truesdales' formal dinner table from Tom listening to their mothers discuss whether to go with sea foam and rose or forest and burgundy shades. Savannah wasn't fond of either.

Partners By Design

The only reason she'd come to this awkward little get together was to land the contract to renovate the Truesdale formal living area into a more serviceable room. And with each glass of wine, their taste seemed to deteriorate.

"If you would like, I could bring over some fabric samples next week," Savannah offered.

Both women ignored her. They'd moved on to discussing the other women in their spin class at the club. It seemed that someone was doing the naughty with someone, who happened to be married to someone else.

Savannah caught Tom's eye, hoping he'd shut the conversation down.

Tom shook his head. "Mother, that stuff has been going on since the beginning of time. Do we have to analyze it at dinner?" He winked at Savannah.

"Well, I was just—"

Savannah grinned back at him.

"To new friendships." Mr. Truesdale raised his wine glass and clinked it against Savannah's. "I believe we're boring this young lady."

"No, I just thought I could get an idea for what you both have in mind for the renovation."

"Certainly, darling." Mrs. Truesdale said. "I was just concerned for the Jones' marriage. They've been together over twenty years."

Partners By Design

"I played a round of golf with Mr. Jones last week and everything seemed fine. How about we let him worry about his marriage?" Mr. Truesdale suggested.

Tom grinned at Savannah. "Welcome to a typical family dinner around the Truesdale table. Who shall we skewer? Our main course tonight is Jones kabob's served up on a bed of satin sheets with a delectable side of infidelity."

"Tom!" His mother scolded. "We aren't skewering anyone."

The cloying mixture of Mom's Estee Lauder and Mrs. Truesdale's Chanel No. 5 had given Savannah a pounding headache. "Please excuse me." She folded her napkin and pushed her chair back so fast she almost took the tablecloth with her. She wound her way through Tom's parents' sprawling Mediterranean home, but before she reached the bathroom, Mom grabbed her elbow.

"What's wrong with you tonight? You're irritable. Ohmygod, Tom Truesdale would be an awesome catch."

"No!" Savannah stopped at the door. "I mean, he's a nice man, but I'm not interested in Tom. And he doesn't seem that interested in me."

Mom tilted her head and studied Savannah. "How can you act so blasé? Tom Truesdale is the most eligible bachelor in this town."

"And I should feel so lucky to be having dinner at his home," Savannah finished her mother's thought. "You have

59

Partners By Design

everything all figured out and we only had one date. He and I don't have a thing in common. There's no spark."

"Be flexible." Constance winked. "If I were a few years younger, I'd go after him myself."

No doubt. Every boyfriend she'd ever brought home had gone goo-goo-eyed over Mom. Except Logan. "I don't have time for a relationship," she protested.

Her mother, Constance as she preferred even her daughters to call her, smoothed her size six gold lamé blouse and twisted at one of her costume earrings. "Savannah, as always I want your happiness above all else, but the situation has never been this bad. The mortgage company is threatening to foreclose on our home."

"Maybe you could find a job." Savannah massaged her temples and tried not to inhale any more pungent perfume.

"What kind of job? I have no marketable skills. After Daddy died, I spent his life insurance educating you girls and on that storybook wedding of Chelsea's." Constance stared up at the ceiling and let out an exasperated sigh. "Sweetie, look at this fabulous house. Old money."

"Mom." Savannah closed her eyes and fought to hide the tension in her voice. Her mother only had her best interest in mind. "I'm not doing this. Not tonight. Not here."

Constance took Savannah's arm, and propelled her outside onto the cobblestone patio. She pressed the tips of her fingers against her neck. "What are we supposed to do? Donald took off and left me two months behind on the mortgage. I cringe when the phone rings because of the creditors. Damn electric company threatening to shut me off. You have school loans. With your sister's husband refusing to help anymore, it's down to you and me, kiddo."

Savannah rubbed her eyes. Losing the house would destroy Mom. In lieu of the woman snaring another rich suitor fast, that left Savannah to come up with the money. And mom was not above using Savannah as bait to catch a husband to save them both.

They both wanted the same thing, security, but they differed in what they were willing to do to obtain it. How ironic that the 'rich man' Constance landed turned out to be as broke as she was and looking for a rich woman to pay *his* bills. Constance had been sucked in by the male version of herself.

Savannah set her purse on the wrought iron table and dug for her checkbook. "If I pay the minimum on my credit card again, I can spare two-hundred. Maybe that will keep your electricity on."

"That's very sweet, but it's just a drop in the bucket." Folding the check and slipping it into her bra, Mom widened her contact-enhanced, emerald green eyes. "You do understand what's at stake here?"

Mom's words resounded like a cell door clanging shut, with Savannah on the wrong side of the bars. She shook her head. "I do, but the best way to fix this is to get my business off the ground. In the meantime, I still have my day job."

Constance straightened a strand of Savannah's hair and stared her in the eye, nodding. "We don't have the luxury of time."

"I know." Savannah nodded her agreement. "Now, we'd better get back before they send out a search party."

* * *

Savannah wasn't sure what to say to Logan Monday afternoon. She'd hung wooden blinds all day in a show home but hadn't come up with any brilliant resolution. Her job at Windows To Go had become so routine it didn't even serve to distract her turbulent thoughts.

Be rational, Savannah. All those emotions Logan awakened yesterday were nothing except an in-your-face resurgence of teenage hormones, like he'd said. If they'd just dated and broken up like a normal couple, she wouldn't even remember his name. But the relationship had ended as abruptly as it started. One night they were making love and planning their forever after and then...nothing.

Judging by yesterday, he wasn't going to tell her what happened without her prying it out syllable by syllable. But knowing would only reopen old wounds and she needed to look forward, not back.

The smartest move to put the past behind them and establish a working relationship was to just keep it

Partners By Design

professional. And the sooner the better.

By the time she finished at Windows To Go, Savannah had convinced herself she had her plan together. She could work both jobs and pull this off. Who was she kidding? That was child's play compared to establishing a professional relationship with Logan.

Logan was already at the office when she arrived. The only way to get through this was to show him that none of that whole lust thing mattered. She had all that in perspective now and their business relationship was just that. She dropped a bundle of brochures in her office and tromped straight to Logan's before she lost her nerve. "Hi."

"Hello." Grabbing a stack of books out of a box, he didn't even look up.

"I really appreciate you getting me the contract with Kathy." Her hands twisted and she rubbed her palm with her thumb.

"Any time." He continued to pull magazines out of the box and stack them on the shelf. "Do you want something, Savannah?"

So he was still bothered about yesterday. For some reason, that appeased her ego. At least he wasn't unscathed. But they had to get past this.

Needing to busy her hands, she reached in the box and fished out a Nerf dartboard and four sponge balls. "What's this?"

Partners By Design

As he glanced up from what he was doing, Logan's short hair fell across his forehead rekindling memories of the longer style he wore in high school. He looked sheepish. "Stress relief."

She squeezed a sponge ball and tried to think of how best to get her point across that she wanted to forget the past. Any angle she took would be awkward, but at least that would help steer them away from the thought of any possible romance. Keep it casual. "Maybe I should make a trip to The Dollar Store."

He took the board and clipped it over the door. "Feel free to try it out before you invest your retirement fund."

Tossing him a yellow ball, she shrugged. "So how does this work?"

He set up the shot and barely missed the bull's-eye. "For every ball that sticks, I let one thing that's bothering me go."

"And that works for you?"

"In theory."

"You're crowding my shot." She pushed him aside and tossed, but her ball didn't stick.

He bumped back. "Flimsy excuse for a lousy aim?"

She ducked and retrieved the ball as it bounced off and rolled across the floor. "This *is* cheaper than therapy." She took another shot and missed the target.

"You ever planning to look at me?" He

64

tossed her the ball and leaned a shoulder against the wall. "Did you have something on your mind?"

"No!" Savannah squeezed the sponge ball until her fingernails dug into her palm. "Maybe, but..."

Back away. Professional. Establish the grounds.

Her hands shook as she snatched the ball off the floor and stepped back. She had to stop this insanity. Don't look at him. Just say it. "Two out of three."

Her haphazard shot flew to the left and hit high on the door just as it opened.

Oh shit!

In excruciating slow motion the bright yellow ball ricocheted off Tom's suit jacket and dropped at his feet. His mother stood beside him, eyebrow cocked.

The only sound was the air conditioner whirring. Mrs. Truesdale frowned at Logan. Logan looked from her to Tom to Savannah. Savannah felt like a naughty third grader caught shooting spit wads while the teacher had stepped out of the classroom.

Her watch showed five past five. She couldn't speak. Thanks to Logan, she'd lost track of time. Even worse. It had actually slipped her mind that Mrs. Truesdale had a five o'clock appointment. How professional.

Tom retrieved the ball and the corners of his mouth turned up. "And here

Partners By Design

I was feeling sorry for you having to pull double duty."

Savannah stepped away from Logan, ignoring his dark scowl. She grinned at Tom, but had no excuse.

"You must be the suite mate." Tom extended his hand to Logan. "Tom Truesdale and my mother, Bridgette."

Logan accepted the handshake, but the scowl remained. "Logan Reid."

Partners By Design

Chapter Six

Logan closed down the design he'd been working on all evening and paced across his living room. Four hours after the fact and the image of Savannah's face when that Don Juan arrived was still embedded in his brain. Like someone had hit pause during the final act in a sappy, melodramatic soap opera.

Definitely more to her uncomfortable reaction than an innocent client relationship. When she'd driven off in that Lexus with Don Juan and his mother, Logan had wanted to put his fist through the wall, or the guy.

He should feel relieved. No need to worry about Savannah getting too close now. Or about him making a fool of himself over a doomed relationship. He should have known a woman like Savannah would be involved with someone.

He tugged on his boxing gloves and threw a couple punches, rewarded with the solid familiarity of frustration absorbing into the bag.

She could have said, "Back off. I have a boyfriend." But no. Hell no. She let him kiss her yesterday. She'd kissed back like he still mattered.

How had he let her suck him in again?

Steadying the bag with both fists, he rested his forehead against it.

Why couldn't he get that long ago night out of his mind?

The first night they met they'd ended up full on making out. He'd taken more cold showers in the two weeks he'd been with Savannah than the rest of his life combined. They'd been two hormonal teenagers. But it had felt like so much more at the time.

Logan gave the bag one last swing, took off his gloves, drained the beer, and tossed the empty bottle into the garbage. Never had any woman cut him so deep and so quick. God, he'd loved her. And then he'd made her hate him. Even now, looking back, her damn mother hadn't left him any choice. The statutory rape threat might be a non-issue now. But even then, that had paled against her bigger threat.

* * *

"My love life, or lack thereof, is none of his business," Savannah said to Mallory after Logan disappeared into his office Tuesday afternoon without so much as a 'Hello.'

Mallory let out a whistle as the door closed with a resounding click. "You think?"

Dinner with Tom and Bridgette Truesdale had been uncomfortable after they'd caught her in a somewhat unprofessional situation, but Savannah could only hope the end result was a contract. As for Logan jumping to the obvious conclusion, she should feel guilty, but she didn't owe him an explanation and if he thought she was involved with someone else, it should help keep him at a distance.

"There is nothing between me and Logan so why should I explain about a non-relationship? How stuck-up would I sound blabbing about something he obviously doesn't care about?" She caught her breath and wrinkled her nose.

Mallory folded her arms. "Uh huh. Well on the flip side, if there is nothing between you, why *not* explain?"

Not a question she had an answer for. "Just...don't..."

Mallory tilted her head then disappeared inside their office, leaving Savannah to stare from one closed door to the other.

Savannah rubbed her eyes. Why hadn't she told him? Really? Had she been testing Logan to see if he'd react? To wonder what she *wasn't* saying? Was it just morbid curiosity to see if the past haunted him like it did her or was she starting to operate like her mother? Anything for a guy's attention. How nauseating was that?

Yeah, and how insane was it to start a business before she had money to back it and still had to hold down a full-time job? She couldn't survive without the steady paycheck. So far they didn't have enough contracts to cover the office expenses, much less day-to-day living.

    The computer clock read eight-fifteen when Savannah shut it down. Mallory had left an hour ago. Logan too, probably. But Savannah had wanted to finish documenting and pricing her ideas for Ms. Truesdale's living room. And she'd promised to email Kat some websites for blinds and preliminary figures to redo her master bedroom.

    Stretching, she slung her purse and computer case over her shoulder, pulled her office door closed, and glanced across the reception area at the sliver of light beneath Logan's door. What horrible thoughts did he have of her?

    She made her way out of the building. Beautiful, clear night, cool enough to roll the van windows down and leave the air conditioner off. Fighting with her emotions, she ran through the drive-thru line at a fast food restaurant to satisfy her growling stomach and on impulse, ordered two sandwiches. Maybe the way to Logan's heart was through his stomach. Not that she wanted into his heart, but a little friendship would make life easier. They had to make peace or sharing a suite was going to be unbearable.

    Logan's truck sat alone in the parking lot when she returned. She grabbed the bag and drinks and let herself into the building. What was the worst he could do? Toss her peace offering in her face?

    She shifted the food, took a deep breath, tapped on his office door, and pushed it open.

Logan glanced from the computer, to her, and landed on the bag in her hand.

She placed the drinks on the coffee table in front of the navy sofa and offered a conciliatory smile. "Figured you had to be starved by this hour."

He stood and ran his hand through his hair. "Thanks."

She let out her breath and sat. "I thought I worked late tonight."

He dropped onto the sofa beside her and accepted the sandwich. "I lost track of time. Again."

Unwrapping her own sandwich, she gathered courage and set her jaw. "As suite mates, just to keep the air clean between us, I'm not involved with Tom Truesdale."

"Your personal life is none of my concern," he snapped.

"That's not what...that isn't why I told you." She waited and then decided his lack of response was as close as she was going to get to approval to continue. "My business comes before everything else." She shrugged. "His mother is a prospective client."

"So you're playing him along?"

So much for making peace. She lowered her eyebrows. "He's a friend."

"So that's how it works for women like you and Connie?" He spat her mother's name like it was poison. "You find some rich guy and play him along until you can squeeze whatever money you can out of the situation?"

"That's not...Wait a minute!" Where did that come from? She stopped herself. Logan seldom vented, and this one seemed out of the blue.

He swallowed a bite and shook his head. "I'm sure Mommy Dearest approves of Mr. Lexus?"

"Care to tell me what you have against my mother?"

His straw squeaked as he jabbed it through the slot in the plastic lid. "Your mother is obsessed with money, status, and control."

She held her tongue. His words sounded far from flattering put in those terms, but there was more than an element of truth to his summation. "Mom is just looking for security."

"What are you looking for?"

Enough. She wrapped her sandwich back in the foil wrapper and stuffed it in the bag, slung her purse over her shoulder, and stomped out the door.

"Savannah." He chased her into the reception area and grabbed her shoulder. "I'm sorry. You were nice enough to bring me dinner and I'm picking a fight."

She rolled her shoulder out of his grasp and spun, but faced with the sincerity in his eyes, she stopped. Her anger dissipated and her arms dropped to her side. "Logan, if we're going to see each other every day we need to get along."

"You're right." He reached out and took the bag from her hand. "Come back and keep me company. Please."

Savannah followed Logan inside the office and sat. "Well, you know all about my lack of a love life. You don't have a girlfriend?" She bit her tongue. None of her business.

"I'll think about that after I graduate in December and get this business going."

"Ah, so you schedule love like you would a construction job?" she asked with a wink. Was he just like her? Allowing his business to push his social life down the priority list? Way down in her case.

He ran a hand through his hair causing little spikes on top and stared at her like he couldn't figure out why she found his approach amusing. "Guess it does sound a little cold."

Not really. Made perfect financial sense. They needed a neutral topic before she asked more prying questions. "What are you working on this late?"

"A bid for a full restoration on a small English Tudor a few blocks from here." He rubbed the nine o'clock stubble on his jaw. "If I don't get it to them this week, I don't have a chance and I need that contract."

She nodded. "It's hard to find time to generate business and get this place going while holding down a day job."

Partners By Design

He scrubbed his hands down his jeans and raised an eyebrow. "The architect I'm interning for is riding me to finish two projects. One's two weeks behind schedule. I've gotta get things lined up or there won't be money to replace the paycheck when I quit in December." He took a drink. "But this Tudor is a dream job. It needs work, but it has two stone porches. Arched brickwork entering the front porch and original wood floors." The exuberance in his voice flowed into her psyche.

"You have pictures?"

He turned his laptop toward her and touched a key. A drawing appeared. "They want to knock out a wall between the kitchen and dining area. Open it up to combine the breakfast nook and formal dining into one large room."

"And the problem is?"

"If I design it the way they have in mind, traffic flow stinks. The only kitchen entrance is through the dining room."

"So add a door here and give them direct access between the living area and kitchen," she suggested, pointing to a wall. Their thighs brushed and she shifted away a couple of inches. She tried to focus as he flipped to the next drawing.

"Except it's a load-bearing wall and has all the wiring for the appliances. Messing with it is going to increase the cost significantly. Not sure how much he plans to sink into the project and I don't want to price myself out of the running."

Partners By Design

She shook her head. "But that's the most livable layout."

"Yeah, and if I extend this wall out, they don't lose any cabinet space. I can duplicate the current archway between the living and dining for the kitchen entrance. Maintain the structural integrity."

She leaned in and focused on the kitchen. "I'd move the fridge over here and position the stove here. The sink should be under the window. Does it have a view?"

"Yard needs work. Couple recently retired. Downsizing." He switched screens and pulled up another folder. "These are shots I took the other day."

Eager to see the house, she reached across him and scrolled through the pictures. His breath stirred her hair, distracting her concentration. "I'd love a chance at remodeling that kitchen, every convenience, but we'd have to stay in the style of the era. Have you seen the great appliances on the market?"

She clicked to go back and a different set of pictures opened. Sketches and architectural drafts of similar type homes, floor plans, even a community layout. "This is cool. One of your current projects?"

He didn't speak as she continued to scroll through them. "I love this. Where is it?" Reality hit. "This is the neighborhood you told me about when you first drove me through TCU. You said you

Partners By Design

were going to design and build a new development with the feel of these homes? Each one with a unique style."

"How the hell did you remember that?"

She remembered every detail about their relationship. A subject a little too intimate for this conversation. "Right location and it'll sell out faster than you can build them."

"If I ever get the money to get it off the ground."

By the time Logan walked Savannah to her van, it was almost midnight. Three hours had flown by in a heartbeat. They read each other's thoughts. His ideas had her designer mind spinning. His closeness had her libido spinning.

She'd never get to sleep tonight.

She waved and crawled into the van, grimacing at the sickening sound of ripping fabric. Her best pair of black slacks. Half her wardrobe was built around them.

She worked the fabric loose from the door handle, stuck the key in the ignition, and glanced at Logan waiting on the sidewalk. He didn't get into his truck until her van started.

* * *

Man, he was wiped. By Friday afternoon, Logan was desperate for a day off, but that wasn't going to happen anytime in the next three months.

He grabbed the notes he'd made at the

Pearson house, locked the truck, and headed into the office. Maybe if he worked up the plans while they were fresh in his mind he could still salvage time to do laundry before Monday.

Savannah sat at the reception desk, surrounded by an assortment of office supplies. It was her turn to cover the phones. They'd discussed hiring a part-time receptionist, but they couldn't afford it until business picked up.

She dropped a handful of pens into the lap drawer and grinned at him, at the same time she grabbed the ringing phone.

At least it was ringing.

"I can't tonight. Got to cover the phone another hour or so and update my books." She paused. "Sounds lovely, but if I don't get these invoices out, we don't get paid."

Logan carried his satchel into his office and dropped it on the desk. Judging from Savannah's tone, someone was insistent.

"I realize meeting people is important for business and I'd love to, but..." She rolled her eyes at Logan when he walked into the reception area. "I know."

The tension had diminished after their truce, but not Logan's awareness of her. Her long legs, her scent, her smile. Maybe if she kept at least ten feet between them. Ten miles might work better.

He wasn't even sure who she was

talking to. "Take off. Do the invoices in the morning. I'll cover the phone."

"Are you sure?" she mouthed, holding one hand over the mouthpiece.

He shrugged. "I'll be here late anyway."

Savannah smiled and put the phone to her ear. "I'll meet you at the club around seven. Bye." She dropped the receiver in the cradle and handed Logan a couple of blue slips. "You got two calls this afternoon. One guy sounds anxious to talk to you about remodeling a house he just inherited. Said a Mr. Pearson gave him your name."

"Thanks."

"Thank *you*," she said, flashing him a killer smile on her way out the door.

Logan sat at the reception desk, trying to forget that he'd just enabled Savannah to go meet some other guy. At least he assumed it was a guy. A guy she might even end up in bed with before the night was over. He needed to do something about his own lack of a love life. His imagination was becoming way too active.

* * *

The weekend was gone before it got started and Logan still had more things left on the list than checked off. He didn't even score a decent night's sleep. Good thing they'd stocked the office kitchen because every weeknight one or all three of them worked late.

Wednesday night, it was after six

Partners By Design

before he made it to the office. Savannah and Mallory had a meeting with a client scheduled and judging by the closed door, it was still underway. Logan docked his laptop, hoping for a couple hours productivity before he went comatose.

He got in almost an hour before Savannah and Mallory distracted him, showing their client out. The door wasn't even closed before the girls raced into his office, both grinning like kids on the last day of school.

"We were thinking pizza," Mallory said. "A third contract, even if it isn't huge, warrants a celebration, don't you think?"

His stomach growled as he stood and stretched. "Any excuse that involves food works for me. We ordering in?"

"Oh yeah. We have a million things to organize and I have to leave early tomorrow night," Mallory said, then turned to Savannah. "Quentin's taking me to the Cattleman's Club."

Logan paid the pizza guy, but when he returned to his office he found Savannah bent over, cleaning off the coffee table. Her slacks rode low on her hips. He blinked at the quick glimpse of her hot pink thong.

Oh lord! Just don't think about her. He gulped and plopped the pizza box on the table. "I'll get napkins."

Mallory grinned. "I've got the

sodas."

Savannah sat cross-legged on the floor, in between bites talking to Mallory about how to bring the new job in on time and within budget. All Logan could think about was that pink thong.

She'd clipped her hair up on top of her head in a mass of curls. Watching her wrap a renegade strand around her finger then release it, Logan tried to keep his fantasies in check as the soft curl caressed her kissable neck. How had he let himself get trapped in this situation? The lady was off limits.

He grinned as Mallory fished a mushroom off his pizza and dropped it in her mouth. She reminded him of his kid sister. "I can stop by that designer fabric store and pick out some samples for the chairs. I know a guy who can cover them and have them back within a week."

"I was figuring on us doing it ourselves," Savannah countered. She dabbed at a spot of pizza sauce on her blouse, drawing his attention to her chest. "It would save a chunk of cash."

If Logan had written the dialogue, he'd have reversed the characters. Cash had never been an issue for the Savannah he remembered, but evidently since her father's death, things had changed.

"Oh, about tomorrow night. You aren't wearing the red silk dress your mom bought you last Christmas?" Mallory asked wiggling her eyebrows.

"To get the invoices out?" Savannah

laughed.

"Good, then you wouldn't mind if I borrowed it?"

Savannah nibbled her bottom lip and fiddled with one of the blue Nerf balls from his dart set. "I think I got rid of that."

"You wore it a couple weeks ago to the Fitzhugh's party," Mallory said.

"Right, but it was really tight." Savannah grinned. "But we're still on for the fair Friday night, right?"

"Absolutely. We can even write it off as a business expense because of the exhibits," Mallory said.

He'd take bets Savannah was making this whole dress thing up as she went along. Yesterday he'd stopped at a sandwich shop down the street and seen Savannah heading into the Resale Boutique wrestling with a huge armload of clothes. He'd thought then that she didn't seem like the resale shop type. Savannah always dressed like a fashion model. And she couldn't need money that bad. Or could she? He'd assumed if they got in a bind, Mommy Dearest would bail Savannah out.

Savannah tossed the ball to him and turned the conversation. "So did you call that guy about the house in Tanglewood Estates?"

He caught the ball and swallowed his bite. "Yeah, I've got an appointment this weekend to tour the house and evaluate our options. He wants to tear out walls and

Partners By Design

build a new family room on the--"

Savannah's cell phone chimed the old bubble gum tune of <u>You and Me Against The World.</u>

She flipped the phone open. "Hi, Mom. You aren't going to believe this!" she gushed. "We landed that...Oh...Oh, I know." The corner of her mouth turned up but the smile didn't reach her eyes. "I can't. Mallory and I are going to the fair Friday night." She pushed her paper plate aside. "We're going to dine on fair food, gorge ourselves on grease and sugar. I know. It'll be fun." A long sobering pause. "Okay."

She flipped the phone shut and forced a smile so sweet even fair food seemed healthy in comparison. "Where were we?"

Chapter Seven

Logan gave up. He had so many things on his to do list, he couldn't keep track. Finally he took Friday afternoon off from the construction site to meet with his new client and catch up on his own business. As he walked into the suite, he overheard the girls in their office.

"Tonight?" Savannah's tone sounded defeated. "I'm sorry. I do understand that Quentin trumps corny dogs. Absolutely. But—this is the last weekend."

"Savannah, I'm really, really sorry. But Quentin's buddy came in a day early and I don't have any option."

"I know. It's just..."

Logan slipped into his own office, but not fast enough to miss her last words. "It's no big deal. Maybe I'll just go by myself."

Oh, now there's a great idea. An attractive female alone at night in south Dallas. He deposited his laptop on the desk and headed to the kitchen for a cold bottle of water, meeting Mallory in the reception area.

"She okay?" he asked.

"You heard?" She smirked. "She's—

Partners By Design

Savannah doesn't make plans often these days so when she does and they fall through, well, you know."

Logan raised an eyebrow. "She can't go by herself."

Mallory frowned. "You know Savannah." She flashed that impish little grin of hers. "Gotta run. Quentin's going to strangle me if I'm late one more time."

Logan waited, debating the wisdom of spending the evening alone with Savannah. He hadn't been distracted by her legs in...well...he hadn't actually seen them since yesterday.

Screw it. He opened the door, and leaned against the doorframe. "I have this sudden craving for a Fletcher's corny dog."

Savannah glanced up from her desk. "Logan, that's very sweet, but you don't have to do this. I know you're busy."

"Yeah, well, after listening to you all week, I have to go. My stomach is screaming for a shot of grease." He picked up her purse and handed it to her. "Besides, if we go to the crafts pavilion we can write it off. You coming?"

She shouldered the purse. "When you put it like that."

* * *

The aroma of fair food wafted across the parking lot before they even made it inside the front gate. Hotdogs, cotton candy, and the tangy smoke from smoldering ribs. Savannah sighed. "My nose is in heaven."

Logan tilted his head and inhaled. "I haven't been here in years. The few times I came, it was always on school field trips. My parents couldn't afford to bring a family of five."

"Mine couldn't afford it either, but they never let that stop them." She looked around, letting the swirling chaos of the Texas State Fair soak into her psyche. "What do I crave most, a corny dog or a funnel cake?"

He made the decision, taking her hand and winding his way past Big Tex and through the crowd toward a corny dog stand.

Lacing her fingers through his, she enjoyed the warmth. "I can't eat too much or I'll get sick on the rides." She held her sweaty hair off her neck and took the sizzling corny dog from him. "It's so muggy. Don't think that cold front is ever going to move through."

"Last weather report I heard, it's supposed to blow in around ten." Logan stopped to drown his corny dog in mustard and ate a third of it in one bite. "So what's the big deal with you and the fair?"

"It started as a family tradition, until Chelsea discovered boys and makeup. So Daddy and I made it our annual excursion. He loved the rides."

Savannah took a bite and listened to the high-pitched symphony of squeals as the roller coaster roared down a steep hill then rumbled past and up the incline for the next series of curves and plunges.

"I'm not riding that, by the way," he said.

"Yeah, you are." She purchased two tickets, pitched her corny dog stick in a trashcan painted with the Texas state flag, and led him toward the line. "Didn't you ride it when you were a kid?"

He narrowed one eye at the towering track. "Once."

As they slung around the first curve, Savannah gripped the rail until her knuckles turned white, anticipating the impending plummet. The metal seat was just wide enough for the two of them and she liked the security of his leg pressed close against hers. Letting go of her frustrations by screaming, she felt as carefree as the kid who'd ridden with her daddy years earlier. Her heart raced and she'd never seen Logan laugh as hard as they slammed around one curve after the other only to plunge straight down and up the next incline.

"This one's even worse than the roller coaster you dragged me on at Six Flags," he said as the train jolted to a stop. The tips of his hair were damp, making it look darker.

As they exited, she grabbed her chest to make sure her heart was still beating. Six Flags. That was the last thing she needed in her mind tonight. Clinging to Logan on the roller coaster. His searching hand beneath her shirt as they made out on

Partners By Design

the boat ride through the cave. Trying on ridiculous cartoon hats and flirting. "Maybe a nice merry-go-round."

"Did you know your phone's playing <u>Don't Worry, Be Happy</u>?" he asked, flagging down a passing vendor carrying pink and blue cotton candy. "What color?"

Ignoring the phone, she pointed. "Pink, of course."

Logan walked backwards a couple steps, peeled off a swatch of sticky cotton candy, and placed it into her mouth. He fell in step beside her. "How about if we check out the Midway and you win me a Kewpie doll?"

She let the feathery glob melt on her tongue and tried not to react to the intimacy of Logan hand feeding her. "You're supposed to win me something, dude." She swiped a strand of pink off his chin.

He popped another piece of cotton candy into his mouth, peeled off a strip, and folded it into hers. "I've never had much skill for tossing pennies in crystal dishes or shooting duckies with cork guns. You're the fair girl. I was counting on you."

"I wouldn't want to insult your male ego by showing you up in front of all those macho types on the midway," Savannah said, taking the last bite of candy and licking the pink sticky sugar off her fingers. "Maybe we should check out the new cars."

They wandered into the showroom and

she went straight to a mid-size SUV. She opened the door and sat, running her hand over the rich tan leather and inhaling the new car scent. "This is what I should buy once the big bucks start rolling in."

Logan read the specs off the sticker. "It's loaded."

"Yeah, and a price tag to match I'm sure. With a little luck my van will hold together for another year or two."

"Same with the truck. It's well used, but it runs." He cocked his head to one side. "You do look good in this thing though."

She tossed her hair over her shoulder, surprised by the unexpected compliment. "Sexier than in a nine year old minivan?"

"The van serves your purpose for now."

Swallowing a lump, she stared at him. "You're the first person to get that. Mal teases me about looking like I'm on the way to carpool some brood of snotty-nosed kids. Mom thinks I drive it just to embarrass her."

The corner of Logan's mouth twitched. "And you don't?"

"Ehh." She smirked. "Maybe a smidge."

They left the showroom and shared a beer and a pretzel, with a powdered sugar-dusted funnel cake for dessert. Her mouth tasted sticky. At this rate they'd both be sick.

The wind gusted and Savannah grabbed her hair and held it away from her face, studying the darkening sky. "Not sure that cold front is going to hold off until ten."

A napkin flew off the bench and Logan stepped on it, bent, and grabbed it. He popped the last bite of funnel cake in his mouth and nodded toward the Creative Arts Pavilion. "Is that where you wanted to go?"

Chill bumps popped out from the sudden cool air on her heated skin and she rubbed her hands up and down her bare arms. The smell of rain permeated the muggy air. "Maybe summer is finally going to let go and give us a little relief from this heat."

A flash of lightening cracked the distant sky and the trees whipped toward the south. "From the looks of those clouds, we're about to get drenched."

Leaves and paper cups swirled through the air like wind-whipped kites. People darted for protection inside the exhibits. Savannah turned her head and let the damp wind toss her hair as electricity crackled through the air. "Maybe we should skip the crafts and head out?"

Logan placed his hand on her back and maneuvered them toward the building. "We won't melt. We're here. Might as well check it out."

People who'd rushed inside to avoid the impending storm milled about the pavilion, examining the assortment of

Partners By Design

crafts and foods. Award winning jams and jellies. Home sewn quilts and delicate crochet. Savannah turned and found Logan beside a bread machine display, talking to a young girl and tasting bread and butter.

He looked irresistible with a five o'clock shadow and windblown hair, tousled like he'd just rolled out of bed.

She shook away the thought and tried not to dwell too far into that image as Logan moved on to a guy serving tiny cups of chili.

Savannah turned her attention to a gorgeous heather green quilt with peach appliqué roses. An entire country bedroom materialized in her mind, all designed around that single piece. Examining the work, she made sure it was hand-stitched. Delicate work. Just the right weight, not too heavy for Texas weather.

She turned the price tag over and winced. Considering the hours that went into it, not that out of line, but still more than she could afford with the business and the check she'd given Mom last Friday.

Logan stepped up behind her and rested one hand on her shoulder. "My grandmother quilted. Hers were a bunch of multi-colored squares she pieced together on her sewing machine. This one's beautiful."

Impressed that he appreciated the craftsmanship, she widened her eyes. "Yeah, but not in my budget."

She fingered the soft cotton and let

the corner drop.

He leaned around. "Anything you covet that much, you should have."

The woman standing behind the table offered a smile. "Nothing like a homemade quilt to snuggle under on a night like tonight."

"Just what I was thinking," Logan said, brushing his lips across Savannah's cheek in a suggestive caress.

Savannah flushed at her body's purely sexual response. She shook off the thought of curling up with Logan in the four-poster bed she'd pictured when she first saw the quilt. This was just a fun night at the fair with a friend. A momentary escape from reality, no more. No future.

But it did feel comfortable. With Logan, it was okay to just be Savannah. She didn't have to squelch her temper. She didn't have to pretend to be a socialite. She'd forgotten what it was like not to have to live the image Mom had worked so hard to create for her.

"That peachy color matches your bedroom walls," he said.

She clamped her mouth shut. He'd made one quick trip to her house helping move furniture for the office and knew what color her bedroom was? "Logan." She said with a raised eyebrow, then smiled at the older woman. "Let me think about it."

Taking his hand, she tugged him away. "You deliberately made her think we were lovers."

Partners By Design

He grinned and reached for a tidbit of toast and jelly off a country blue platter. "You should buy the quilt. I've never seen such a wistful look." He took a bite and placed the other half in her mouth. "Your phone's playing <u>You and Me Against the World</u>."

She dug the phone out of her purse and switched it to vibrate. Her mother was not going to ruin the first night Savannah had taken for herself in, well in too long.

She gave the quilt a long look. "I'll be kicking myself for years if I go home without it."

Walking away, with the quilt packed inside a plastic bag, she couldn't stop grinning. "I can't believe you talked her down a hundred dollars. You had her eating out of your hand. She looked at you like she wanted to snuggle under this quilt with you."

His dimples flashed. "Get your mind out of the gutter, woman. She's older than my mom. She wanted to serve me hot chocolate and tuck me in for the night."

"I guarantee any chocolate in her mind involved something kinky." She turned and pressed her back against the pavilion door, but the wind pushed back. Logan leaned around and helped push it open, only to be greeted by a sheet of cold, blowing rain.

"Whoa." He frowned at the dark, rolling clouds and wrapped his arm around her. "That's what my grandmother called a gully washer."

Savannah hugged the quilt to her chest and shivered. "We're going to get soaked."

"Want to go back inside and see if it blows over?" he suggested.

"Looks like it's here for the duration. Let's make a run for it."

Logan pulled her tight and they darted toward the main gate, but everyone else had the same idea. The wind whipped Savannah's hair while icy drops pelted her face. She squealed as a car splashed muddy water over her slacks.

Grasping Logan's hand, she raced across the parking lot toward the truck. The puddles sucked at her sodden loafers. Horns honked and traffic sat at a standstill as they weaved their way through bumper-to-bumper cars full of people fleeing the waterlogged fairgrounds.

When he opened the pickup door, Savannah jumped in, dropped her bag in the floorboard, and held the door open just far enough to remove her shoes and dump the water out. She slammed the door and wrapped her arms across her chest, still grinning like a loon as Logan climbed in the driver's side. His hair dripped in his face and his white shirt was transparent and plastered to his chest.

"Boy, did I get my wish. I'm freezing," she said through chattering teeth, pulling her soaked blouse away from

Partners By Design

her skin.

"Hold on." He dug a duffle bag out from behind the seat and handed her a soft flannel shirt, keeping a pair of jeans for himself. He tilted his head and narrowed one eye. "You're enjoying this."

"Weird, I know, but it's a blast."

His chuckle heated her frozen blood. She hadn't relaxed and had fun like this since...since before Daddy died. Tossing Logan's dry shirt on the dash, she paused at the first button on her blouse. Could she just strip and put on his shirt? Right here in the intimate confines of a pickup cab?

Sheets of rain cascaded down the windows and wind whistled through the miniscule cracks where the window didn't seal. One good thing about parking on the last row of the lot, there were no streetlamps.

"I'll face this door and you face that one." She turned her back and yanked off her shirt and bra and slipped her arms into Logan's dry, flannel shirt. She heard his zipper and the truck rocked as he struggled to peel the wet denim down his legs.

Keep your mind on your own predicament. She added her drippy slacks to the soggy heap on the floorboard.

A flash of lightning lit the cab as Logan shifted positions. "Bear with me here, but I can't get these on without straightening my legs."

Savannah swallowed and tried to ignore the two hairy, muscled calves that appeared on her side of the floorboard. His shoulder brushed against her back as he leaned forward to struggle into the jeans. The closer he moved, the weaker she felt. So distracted, she forgot to finish buttoning the shirt until Logan sat up.

He left one leg stretched across the cab and folded the other beneath him, pulling her back against his chest and scrubbing his hands over her arms. "Warming up?"

She held her breath.

His hands worked like heaters and her body temperature ignited at his touch. Was he aware of the effect? If he didn't stop, she might turn in his arms and devour him. Was her resistance strong enough *not* to climb in his lap and make love to him?

As his hands slowed, she waited for his next move. Would he steal his warmth away and drive her home? Or would he touch her? Please. *Please, let him want me like I want him.*

"Savannah," he whispered.

Partners By Design

Chapter Eight

What? What did he want from her? She strained her neck to study his face, decipher his thoughts. Navy blue eyes burned into hers, but he waited. Why didn't he touch her?

I shouldn't want him to touch me.

His hands were inches from where her shirt gaped open. If she turned just slightly.

Tilting her head against his shoulder, she nuzzled in and rubbed her nose against his neck, inhaling a whiff of rain, sweat, and musky aftershave.

We can't do this.

Don't turn me away.

His mouth covered hers, lips parted, inviting her inside the warmth. His fingers undid the two buttons she'd managed to fasten on the shirt then squeezed her breast. He slid his other hand beneath her hair, his fingers pressing hot as he repositioned her for a deeper kiss.

She tugged on his damp hair, pulling him closer and feasting on his mouth, starved for the once-familiar taste of Logan. His late night shadow scratched her chin and ignited her piqued senses.

Thunder rumbled and clashed across the sky and sheets of rain washed over the truck. Deep in the floorboard her phone vibrated, but she tuned it out.

Logan tasted so right. The years melted away. She was sixteen again, and carefree, and alive. She'd missed this. Missed him.

Logan Reid was the long awaited sequel to her own personal teenage love story. The one she'd replayed in her mind so many times she'd never forgotten a single line of dialogue or erotic sensation. But she'd rewritten the ending hundreds of times.

"Come home with me."

Her eyes popped open and she blinked at Logan. Familiar yes, but not the young boy of her fantasies.

They weren't teenagers and she was not going to let him destroy her again. In desperation, she pushed away and tugged her shirt together. "What made me ever think we could be friends?"

Circling her waist with his hands, he pulled her back against his bare chest, and rested his chin on top of her head. "You were the best friend I ever had, Savannah." His lips nibbled her ear and his breath tickled her neck. "You were everything good that ever happened to me."

His words cut deep into her memories. She'd felt the same. But that was before he'd left her cold and alone with not a single word of explanation beyond, 'It's over.'

She sat up and turned in the seat to face him, putting distance between them. Logan had the power to consume her body and soul and she couldn't risk her heart again and let that happen. "I'm not doing this."

Logan couldn't be counted on. And at the moment, her knowledge of the capacity he had to hurt her was her only defense against falling back under his spell.

The pulsating storm rocked the truck and the windows fogged, transforming the cab into a steamy sauna. Sitting back in the seat, he gripped the steering wheel until the color drained from his knuckles. "You can't convince me this is over."

Fumbling with the buttons on her shirt, she avoided his eyes. What was she supposed to say? I don't want to be in love with you because you scare the crap out of me? "Logan, stop. We both have business to focus on."

The rain ran down the windshield in sheets and Logan's jaw turned to granite. "So no time for relationships," he persisted, turning and sliding his palm down her cheek in a gentle caress. "Look at me, Savannah. Convince me you don't feel it and I'll back away."

Gulping, she set her jaw to match his. "I don't have to convince you."

After a full minute of an intense, pleading glare, he turned away and started the pickup.

When Logan dropped her at the house, Savannah gathered her dripping clothes from the floorboard, wrapped the quilt tightly in the plastic and crawled out of the truck without a word.

She raced onto the front porch as rain dripped off the eaves and pattered against the stone steps. But the pickup stayed in the drive until she opened the front door. She clutched her soggy clothes in one hand and fought the heavy door with the other as Logan's truck backed out of her drive.

She was still in a fog when she entered and found Mallory standing in the kitchen doorway.

Dropping her purse and wet clothes on the floor, Savannah grinned at Mal's Betty Boop nightshirt. "Cool PJs."

"Not as intriguing as your trend setting ensemble," Mallory said with a wink.

Savannah's face heated. "We got rained out."

"Love the shirt, but wouldn't one of those little plastic ponchos have been more practical?" Mallory walked toward her, grinning as if she knew what Savannah didn't have on beneath Logan's shirt.

Savannah tossed the quilt on the couch. "Don't be funny."

"Logan's I presume?" Mallory fingered the flannel work shirt. "Ohmygod, you have to tell me everything."

Partners By Design

Savannah retrieved her wet clothes, traipsed into the laundry room, and stuffed them in the washer. Lowering the lid, she tried to rationalize her raw emotions.

Dogging her heels, Mallory didn't cut her any slack. "Oh come on."

"There's nothing to tell."

Mallory stopped in the door. "Seriously?"

Cold reality began to penetrate, but Savannah needed to talk this out with someone before she exploded. "I'm so furious with myself. He pushed hard, but if I hadn't gotten my libido under control, I'd have been making out with him in the cab of his pickup like two teenagers on prom night."

Clapping her hands, Mallory danced across the kitchen. "What's wrong with that? Logan's a great guy." She pirouetted to a stop. "Oh. The elusive past?"

Savannah massaged her temples. "Yeah, oh." She grabbed a mug from the cabinet, filled it with milk, and stuck it in the microwave. How could her future have been so clear, so well planned a few weeks ago and now everything seemed...unsettled? How could she face Logan after this?

Mallory pulled out a second mug and took the gallon of milk.

"Why can't I love someone like say, Tom?" Savannah continued. "He treats me like a princess."

"True enough, but none of that has

anything to do with what happened tonight."

Her friend sounded too much like Logan. Savannah massaged her temples. "I meet these perfect guys, but as hard as I try, I feel nothing."

"Spontaneity not exactly in the country club types wheelhouses?" Mal asked.

Savannah stared at the ceiling and blinked back stupid, irrational tears. The problem was not them. It was her inability to become emotionally involved. She wasn't convinced that her emotions hadn't slipped into that grave with her father. She'd tuned all her own needs out when responsibility had been forced on her.

"What about Logan?" Mallory coaxed.

"All we have is senseless lust. I can't think clearly around him any more than I could when I was sixteen." Savannah chewed her thumbnail. "Have you ever felt an irrational pull toward someone? If we're anywhere in the same proximity, I just sort of end up right against him. That sounds stupid."

"Sounds intense."

Savannah touched her tongue to her top lip. "Kissing Logan is like, like curling my toes into wet sand. I just want to burrow deeper. I lose all judgment." She couldn't allow herself to go there again.

"Oh, I understand." Mallory took a couple spoons from the drawer and fidgeted, placing them on the counter then rearranging them. "Which is a lead-in to my news. You're going to think I'm a traitor, but--" She jabbed her hands through her short hair. "I'm getting married."

"What?" Though Mallory spent every weekend with Quentin, Savannah had no idea things had progressed to the point of marriage.

"And the kicker is that we're doing it next month."

Savannah's stomach fell to her feet. "Next month?"

"And I'm moving to Quentin's ranch in Oklahoma. We've been talking about it for awhile, but he didn't pop the question until tonight. I mean, we've been together two years." Mallory clasped Savannah's hands between hers. "He's the one. I just know it. I was raised on a ranch. It's in my blood. I've always been a horse girl."

Savannah's legs gave way and she dropped onto a chair. "Oklahoma?"

"I feel like a pile of cow dung doing this just as we're trying to get the business going. But now with you and Logan maybe hooking up, you two can work it out. Right? I'd just be a third wheel."

"There is no me and Logan." Savannah squeezed her best friend's hand. "But of course I'm happy for you. Quentin is your perfect match."

"Is this going to put too much of a strain on you financially?"

Partners By Design

Mallory knew she was scraping by, they both were. But Mallory thought they were doing it because of the challenge to make it on their own. She had her parents to fall back on and Savannah hadn't told her that not only was there no money to fund her, but she was also half supporting Mom again.

"I'll figure it out. Maybe find another partner. Always options if you keep an open mind." Her happy tone sounded forced, even to her.

Even if she landed more clients, it would take months before enough money started coming in to cover the expenses. Still, she didn't have the heart to cloud this magical time in Mallory's life. She stood and wrapped her arms around Mallory. "I'm so happy for you."

"I'm glad, because you're my maid of honor. You look good in magenta, right?"

"I'm honored." Clueless where she'd come up with money to pay for a bridesmaid dress, and a bachelorette party, and an awesome wedding gift, but honored.

Savannah jumped as the phone jarred her out of the moment.

Mallory clasped her hand over her mouth and started toward the phone. "Oh! I forgot. You distracted me with your fashion statement. Your mother has called every half hour. She's like freaking out. Said to have you call the second you got in, no matter how late."

Savannah grabbed her hand. "Don't answer it. It's almost midnight."

Partners By Design

Savannah waited until the phone quieted then took the sticky bottle of chocolate syrup from the fridge and squirted it into her mug. "My cell's been ringing all night, but I just let it roll to voicemail. I can't deal with her mama drama tonight."

"She sounded frantic the last time she called, if that matters," Mallory said.

Savannah popped the cold mug into the microwave and wrapped her hands around the other, absorbing the warmth. She set it in front of Mallory. "I'll check my cell in a minute and see if she left a message."

"Okay."

"Where did you tell her I was?"

"At the fair with friends." Mallory grabbed her mug and started toward the bedroom, but picked up Savannah's DVD of <u>Rebel Without a Cause</u> off the top of the TV as she passed. "You and your bad boys," she said with a grin, laying it back on top of the TV.

Savannah shook her head. "What can I say? James Dean was a hottie."

"So is Logan Reid."

Savannah wrinkled her nose at Malory's departing figure. "So is Tom Truesdale." God, she wished she believed that.

While waiting on the microwave to beep, she checked her cell messages. All Mom said was to call her. It could wait. She finished her hot chocolate, and fell

Partners By Design

into bed, but her brain was too chaotic to sleep. The business was sunk, bankrupt before it even got off the ground. And what about Logan's business? He couldn't afford the suite on his own or he wouldn't have leased half the office to begin with. She rolled over and snuggled into her pillow, listening to the rain pelt the roof.

And their relationship? What relationship? Logan who could still heat her blood to boiling with no more than a raised eyebrow. But one hot kiss did not make a relationship.

Her life was going down the tubes, both romantically and professionally.

At least Mallory was paying her half of the expenses through November. Maybe Logan could sub-lease the entire space and find a cheaper office for his architectural firm. And that would be for the best all around. She could--what? Work for 'Windows to Go' until she was too teetery to climb a ladder?

She crawled out of bed and picked up <u>Rebel Without a Cause</u>. Laying it aside, she plugged <u>Giant</u> into the DVD player instead. What she needed was a magician to pull a lucky rabbit out of a hat. A rich rabbit. A rich rabbit willing to toss a ton of cash her way. The craziest part was that she knew a rabbit, so to speak. And he was perfect. And he wanted to start a relationship and had the ability to make all her problems vanish with the wave of his magic checkbook.

She fast-forwarded past Rabbit--err,

Partners By Design

Rock Hudson and snuggled into the country quilt and James Dean.

She'd never even believed in the Easter Bunny.

* * *

By morning, the rain had drifted east, leaving everything fresh washed and a fall chill in the air. If she didn't have so much to do, Savannah would put off work in favor of a long walk in the crisp air. Clear the turmoil from her mind. At least Mom hadn't been home when she'd called, because one more thing might put her over the edge.

She looked around to make sure Logan's truck wasn't there yet and stepped over a puddle to reach the sidewalk. What could she say to him? *I burn for your touch, but I don't trust you as far as I can throw your tight little butt.* Her pitiful life had come down to two choices. Marry some rich guy like Tom Truesdale and make the best of a loveless marriage or cling to her dream of independence and starve struggling to pay bills the rest of her life.

Her body longed for Logan. Her mind longed for financial independence. And her mother longed to marry her to a man who could pay their bills.

But Savannah wasn't buying into Mom's plan.

She booted up the computer, opened the designs for the new sunroom, and tried to focus. Maybe if she worked longer hours, she could pull in the contract ahead of schedule and even get a referral for more business.

　　Two hours later her ringing cell phone saved her from a website for over-priced wood flooring. She'd completed the proposal for the sunroom, sent out the two invoices for her existing clients, and was considering just going home and catching up on some long overdue sleep. "Hello. This is Savannah."

　　Mrs. Truesdale's voice took her by surprise. "Hi dear. I received the other bid on the living room and wanted to touch base with you before I make a decision."

　　"Another bid?" She stared at the computer screen. "I'm almost done."

　　"If you're free, we could hit a couple fabric stores I found."

　　Not today. "That would be lovely, Mrs. Truesdale, but how about I finish the design and get it to you by the first of next week? Then we can discuss actual fabric."

　　"Okay. I guess I'm just trying to rush things. Patience has never been my strong suit."

　　"No, I should have had it to you by the end of this week." She heard the front door open and wondered if it was Mallory or Logan. "Mrs. Truesdale, I promise, Monday, close of business. I hate to rush off, but someone just came in the office."

　　"Look forward to hearing from you."

　　Savannah rubbed her eyes and walked to her office door. "It's about time

Partners By Design

someone sho-"

"Good morning, sweetie." Her mother pushed her tortoise shell sunglasses up on top of her head and surveyed the office.

Savannah's eyes widened as Tom strolled in behind her.

"Your mom insisted on stopping by this morning," he said.

"Don't be silly." Constance swatted at his hand like a teenager flirting with the high school jock. "I just grew tired of waiting for a personal invitation." She glided across and air-kissed both Savannah's cheeks. Truth was Constance Holt could pass for her sister easier than she could her mother.

"So this is the new office. Quaint, but classy."

"Sorry, I know it was my day to open up." Logan bumped the door shut behind him, juggling blueprints, his laptop, and his tool bag. "Had an emergency with a building inspector at one of the jobsites."

Mom's smile vanished and her plucked eyebrows shot up as her gaze scaled Logan like he was scum on the bottom of his work boots. She pasted that I'm-better-than-you-but-I'll-stoop-to-tolerate-you grin on her peach glossed lips and cocked one hip. Mom had always hated Logan for breaking Savannah's heart. "It's been a long time, Mr. Reid."

He set his tool bag on the receptionist desk and leveled a cold stare

Partners By Design

on her. "Mrs. Holt," he said through gritted teeth.

The fall chill outside felt like a summer heat wave in comparison to the tension in the office. Evidently, Mom had fulfilled her social obligation, because she turned her back almost before he finished speaking. "Savannah, Tom thinks a new BMW would be a smart replacement for that disreputable minivan of yours."

Oh, and did Tom plan to also pay for said BMW? "Mom, my van is fine."

Tom stepped forward and handed her a glossy brochure. "We get a fleet deal for the company. The lease wouldn't be too expensive."

"I appreciate your concern, but when I can afford a new vehicle, I'll buy one."

"Darling," Mom said. "I worry about that heap breaking down and leaving you stranded on some out of the way road."

"Do it for your mom," Tom urged. "Logan, tell her it's dangerous for a single female to be out in that old vehicle."

"Her van, her choice." Logan hauled his stuff into his office and closed the door, a little too loudly to qualify as just closing.

Mom rolled her eyes and huffed, then sashayed into Savannah's office without another glance Logan's way.

Partners By Design

Chapter Nine

Men! Granted, her mother tended to treat people she didn't like with the tiniest hint of condescension. Okay, maybe a giant dose of condescension. Even so, Logan didn't have to slam the door on them. But then again, after their argument last night... She squinted at his door and joined her mother and Tom. "I'm a little confused to see you two together."

Tom held a chair for Constance before crossing the room and holding out Savannah's. "Your mother called me last night, distraught. You didn't answer your cell and she could tell Mallory was covering for something. She thought you might have been with me."

"I couldn't close my eyes all night." Constance rubbed her eyes melodramatically, without even touching them.

Savannah sat at her desk and frowned at her mother, recognizing her ploy to keep Tom Truesdale in the picture. "Mallory has no reason to lie. What had you so upset?"

"Oh, it's horrible." Constance ran her fingers through her hair. "That monster your sister married is dragging

Partners By Design

her off to Chicago."

Monster? When Chelsea married Jared, her mother had raved about the merits of having a successful lawyer in the family.

"Jared and Chelsea are moving?" Savannah took a second to digest the new turn of events. "Okay, so we'll miss having her close by, but that's not the end of the world."

Constance exchanged glances with Tom as if Savannah was a clueless child. "She doesn't want to leave us. He's forcing her to go." She swiped at a non-existent tear.

Tom patted Constance's hand and handed her a handkerchief. "It's not so bad."

Savannah glanced at him, then turned back to her mother. "You can't be this upset over them moving. Knowing Jared, it's some amazing job opportunity and he'll earn a fortune."

"He made her choose between him and me. Completely cutting me off from my daughter."

Given the current situation, cutting Constance off from Jared's financial support was more the plan. "I'm sure Chelsea will bring him around. Jared's not a bad guy."

"Not a bad guy? Listen to what you're saying." Constance paused the conversation long enough to blot her forehead with the linen handkerchief. "Oh I just don't know what I'll do without my little girl."

Savannah gnashed her teeth.

Tom kept one eye on Constance. "We'll talk over lunch. I can help. My mother is waiting at the club."

Lunch? "Tom, I appreciate your gracious offer, but this is not your problem." Savannah turned from him and stared into her mother's green eyes and for the first time recognized raw fear. As Tom's fingers closed over Savannah's shoulder, the cold claws of her mother's dire circumstances closed around Savannah's world.

* * *

Savannah poked her chicken Caesar salad with a fork and swallowed the bite without tasting it. Dishes clattered as club patrons chatted over lunch. And Tom catered to both his mother and Savannah's. She wasn't in the mood to listen to the two older women chatter today, but to make it worse, Mom continued to play the role of distressed damsel. A tactic that had always rewarded her with her every desire from Daddy.

When the two mothers excused themselves to visit with another group of women who'd just arrived, Savannah turned to Tom. "You do know that our mothers are accomplices in a plot to get us together, right?"

He grinned. "You make it sound like a fate worse than death."

"Not at all." She shook her head and grinned. "Look, I appreciate your offer to help, but Mom and I will work this out. She had no business dragging you into our problems."

He took her hand in his, caressing it like fragile porcelain. "She's a friend of my mom's and in need."

"But--"

He leaned across and met her eyes. "Your mother is no different than mine. I understand pampered women." His smile warmed. "It's you I can't figure out. Do you know how sexy you are playing hard to get?"

"This isn't a game," Savannah stated distinctly. "I don't have the time or inclination to add one more thing to my plate."

"I do believe you're serious." He took a deep breath and flashed perfect, white teeth. "Make you a deal. I'll back off, if you'll give me one valid reason you can't have both a career and a relationship."

"Because I have to prove that I can take care of myself." She searched his dark eyes and charming smile, but whatever understanding she craved wasn't there.

He started to touch her face, but evidently thought better of it. "You fascinate me. Most women long to be cared for," he said with a wink.

"It's my career. I have to stand on my own feet or what's the point?" Her own mother didn't understand that the success of this business would prove that she could survive on her own, but Tom was a business man. He should get it. Financial

Partners By Design

independence insured that it would be Savannah's choice what man to be with, or whether to be with a man at all. Being with a man for necessity always ended in disaster.

Savannah blinked as a twisted thought hit her. If Tom were fifteen years older, he really would be perfect for Constance. He might be anyway for that matter. She looked up and realized he was just sitting there grinning at her.

"If the problem is your business, then I should point out that you're going about this all wrong." He waved at a couple as they passed. "I know lots of people I can introduce you to. Contacts, my dear, are the key. Give me a chance. If it ends up being just business, then we both still come out ahead. Part as friends. You earn some good contacts and I get the pleasure of your company."

She couldn't come up with a decent argument. Tom knew almost everyone. And according to her mother, had a different arm candy every week. "Okay." She felt a little sheepish. "It could be a good deal all around, fun. But just so we're clear, I won't have you paying Mom's or my bills. That's not negotiable."

"Done." He winked. "You drive a hard bargain."

She saw her mother disappear into the lady's room. "Excuse me. I should check on Mom."

She wove her way to the restroom. Constance stood in front of the gold leaf framed mirror, perfecting her lips.

She didn't wait for Savannah to initiate the conversation. "I cannot believe you are sharing an office with that Reid boy! Don't tell me you're seeing him again. Not after what he did to you." No trace of the whiney, upset mother from five minutes earlier.

"No, but..." Savannah checked to be sure there was nobody in either of the two stalls.

Constance clicked her lip-gloss shut and whirled on her. "Savannah, grow up. We can't afford idealism. Our family is in dire straits. It would destroy us for you to throw your future away on that blue collar nobody. Logan Reid represents everything I've busted my ass to protect you from." She snapped her purse and wagged a finger in Savannah's face. "Tom Truesdale is your best shot at having that wonderful life I've always dreamed of for you."

"Logan is an architect with a promising future." Not that she planned a future with him, but he wasn't what her mother thought he was.

"A piece of paper is a far cry from making a man successful. The man drives a pickup and holds down multiple jobs just to survive. Hardly the life you've been groomed for. Is it wrong for a mother to want more for her daughter?"

Savannah realized her mother's background clouded her perspective, but still, it wasn't her life. "Now you're faulting his work ethic?"

"Oh for Cripe's sake, Savannah. I know more about hormones than breathing. Don't think I didn't recognize that dazed look in your eyes when you came home three hours past curfew that night."

Savannah gulped, remembering the Sunday eight years ago she and Logan spent at the lake house. "I was sixteen."

"And he was eighteen and sniffing around for sex. You knew what kind of family he was from. The last thing we needed was for you to get pregnant and sucked down into that pit."

A surge of resentment welled up in Savannah. She didn't care for this bitter side of her mother.

She was a grown woman and frustrated with playing the dutiful daughter. And that's what it boiled down to. "Just so you aren't confused. It's not up to you to decide who I see. I support myself and base my relationships on feelings, not finances."

Constance grabbed her arm before she could escape into a stall. "So screw Logan's brains out. Get him out of your system. But then wise up. Settle down and marry Tom."

Savannah wrenched out of her grasp. "Are you serious?"

"Do you want to be responsible for me losing everything?"

"No, Mother, I don't. But don't you see anything wrong with marrying someone for money? What does that make me?" More like her sister and mother than she'd ever dreamed.

"Tom represents so much more than money. The man is infatuated with you. That nonchalant attitude of yours is working. But it's time to give him a shot. If Logan hadn't shown up again, you would not be acting this way."

After her mother's little temper tantrum, Savannah almost reconsidered her agreement to see Tom simply because she really had no desire to give Constance Holt even a morsel of pleasure. "I'm not interested in Logan. If it makes you feel better, I just agreed to give Tom another chance." Savannah closed her eyes and shut the stall door, sliding the latch into place with a click. Mom had been strapped for cash since Daddy's death, but never this desperate. Still, finances weren't going to dictate Savannah's choice in a husband.

Tom was a nice man and she admired his honest approach to dating. He seemed genuinely happy about helping her enhance her contacts. So far she felt nothing for him, but possibly that could change. Either way, as long as she didn't let him pay her bills or Mom's what was the problem? And if she were honest with herself, Tom could provide a badly needed diversion from Logan.

It wasn't like she was in love with Logan. It was just that being with him awakened old emotions. But if Mom was right, and she typically was about men, you could never recreate the excitement of first love. It was plain foolishness to try. But what if it had been true love? Could she ever put it behind her unless she found out?

* * *

Savannah saw her lunch companions off and headed straight to her office to call her sister. How could Chelsea leave her to deal with all this alone?

She punched in the number and waited. One, two, three, four rings before Chelsea picked up. "Hey, Vannah."

Oh, the dreaded nickname. "Hi, Chels." Savannah twisted the cord around her finger and forced her voice to stay calm. "What's this about Chicago?"

"The more important question is what's this about you working with Logan Reid? Are you insane?"

The muscles in Savannah's neck tightened. So Mom had already gathered her allies. "I didn't call to discuss Logan."

"Play your cards to win, little sister. Get far away from him before he drags you down."

"You don't even know him." One speech per day on the merits of marrying for money was her limit.

"You were smart enough to dump Logan in high school. Don't develop a case of the stupids now."

"Actually, he dumped me." Savannah's chicken salad threatened to make another appearance. "And contrary to popular consensus, I am quite capable of making my own choices. Before I throw this phone across the room, let's discuss Chicago."

"Jared landed an impressive position with a top law firm. An old college frat brother." Chelsea's voice lightened as if she hadn't been acting like the world's biggest bitch seconds before. "Chicago! Can you believe it? Museums, theater, restaurants. It'll be amazing."

Savannah dug her nails into her palm at her sister's lack of responsibility. "And you're just going to leave me on my own to support Mom? Dad wanted us to stick together."

The phone was quiet a few seconds. "You'll handle things. You always do."

Savannah hated the vulnerability in her own voice. "I can't afford Mom on my salary. You know how she burns through cash."

"Oh come on. You're the one with the brains and the career. All I have is a useless art history degree and Jared."

"A very expensive, useless art history degree that Mom paid for with money she could be using to support herself."

"I never asked her to put me through SMU," Chelsea said. "Jared's done with Mom and I can't fight him on this or you'll be supporting me too. Do you have any idea how much cash we've poured into Mom's poor choices?"

Partners By Design

"Is this Jared's take on tough love?" Savannah asked, trying not to panic.

Chelsea took a deep breath. "I have to follow my husband. This is a wise career move for him."

Hearing Savannah's raised, shaky voice, Logan came out of his office and grabbed her mail off the receptionist desk, unsure of their relationship after the night before. Yet putting off facing her wouldn't buy anything.

Savannah had her back to the door, leaning against her desk and staring out the window. "I understand it's a great opportunity for Jared."

Realizing she was on the phone, Logan started to leave. But when Savannah reached over and crumpled a piece of paper on her desk, he stopped. Her voice cracked. "So what am I supposed to do, Chels?"

Her shoulders slumped and she shook her head. "Of course I understand. He's your husband."

She softly placed the phone in the cradle and clutched the desktop with both hands. "Damn! Damn! Damn!"

Should he leave...? Before he decided, she turned and caught him standing in the door. Not a word, just a blank, desperate stare. But her chin quivered.

Walking toward her, he reached out one hand. She didn't react so he ran it across her cheek. "What's wrong?"

Savannah stiffened and stepped away. "Don't. This doesn't concern you." She snatched her purse off the desk and moved around him.

What the--? Logan followed her into the reception area and positioned himself between her and the exit. "Is it Truesdale?"

"None of your concern."

"You shouldn't be behind the wheel of a car until you settle down."

Her eyes flashed fury. "Back off!"

He clenched his fists and watched her storm out, slamming the door in her wake. Last night she'd been in his arms. Even though she'd pushed him away in the end, her initial heat proved there sure as hell was something there. Then today, after returning from lunch with Truesdale, she snapped Logan's head off. He stomped into his office and kicked his empty laptop case against the far wall. How did he let her pull him in? Time after damn time.

Concentrate. His mind spun in angry chaos causing him to trash a design he'd been working on all morning. How could she not see what they were doing to her? Her mother. Her sister. Jackass Truesdale! Gritting his teeth, he shut down the PC. Clients weren't knocking their door down anyway. If he worked from home, at least he wouldn't have to worry about seeing Savannah.

He packed his computer and was about

to lock the suite when the phone rang. He grabbed the extension on the receptionist desk.

"Hey, big brother. Nathan's cooking seafood gumbo tomorrow." Kathy's cheery mood only worsened his. "What're the chances of you and Savannah driving out for lunch?"

"Savannah who?" Logan slammed the phone down.

Partners By Design

Chapter Ten

As mind games went, Savannah's stunk. Logan wasn't into this hot and cold crap. Her actions implied that she was with Truesdale. Her body heated to Logan's.

He pushed the phone out of the way and made a second attempt to leave at the same time Mallory shouldered her way into the office.

"Can you grab this?" she asked, shuffling an armload of plastic garment bags and department store sacks. "Wait until you see."

He took the bags out of her hand and followed her back into the room.

She piled her load of treasures on the desk.

"Did Savannah tell you my news?" Her short blond hair stuck out at odd angles and her eyes sparkled. "Where is she?"

"How the hell should I know? Not my day to watch her." Logan dropped the bags on the desk beside the other purchases.

Mallory stopped digging through the bags and stared at him. "Trouble in paradise?"

He ignored the question. "I've got my cell if anyone is looking for me."

Partners By Design

"Did you and Savannah fight?" She sauntered into the kitchen, ignoring the fact that he was trying to leave. She returned gulping a bottle of water.

"She left in a pissy mood." He and Savannah were none of her business. What was he saying? There was no he and Savannah.

"Probably a teensy bit my fault." She pulled the receptionist chair around and dropped like she'd just finished running a marathon. "I'm getting married the end of November."

"Congratulations." What did Mallory's engagement have to do with Savannah's irrational temper? "She doesn't want you to get married?"

Mallory rolled the frosty water bottle across her forehead and let out a breath. "Roommates. Business partners. Me moving to Oklahoma is going to put a serious crimp in her finances."

Logan set his laptop down. "So she's really hurting that bad?"

"She doesn't talk about it, but yeah, things are tight."

"Sorry I snapped at you." He sighed and slung his laptop over his shoulder. "Congrats on your engagement. See you Monday."

Climbing into his truck, he tossed the laptop on the seat and noticed something stuffed in the crack between the cushions. He crooked a finger under the strap and pulled out a pink, lacy bra.

Partners By Design

"Dammit!"

He opened the glove box and added it to Savannah's hair clip from the lake and slammed the door, but it popped back open from the force. He gave it a solid punch then massaged his knuckles. The woman was intent on driving him insane.

* * *

"Is this new?" Savannah asked, taking a seat in a cerulean blue chair in her mother's living room.

"Oh, it's nothing. I bought it before Donald moved out."

Savannah accepted the glass of hibiscus tea and ran her other hand over the brocade upholstery. Not your discount variety. "So he bought it for you?"

"He was helping cover my credit cards at the time. How was I to know he was planning to take a hike?"

One more item on a maxed-out card. The woman had no concept of living within her means. And Donald had been just like her. Savannah nibbled her lip. Hopefully Tom could introduce Savannah to prospective clients and she'd be able to make enough money to save both her business and Mom's house.

And it better happen fast!

Constance raised her glass. "How long are you planning to keep me in suspense? I presume you didn't suddenly realize how much I'll miss Chelsea and decide to spend a relaxing Sunday afternoon keeping your mother company."

Partners By Design

"We've got a problem." Savannah swallowed the subtle barb and chose her words. She'd scrutinized the budget over and over the past couple days, but she couldn't even rob Peter to pay Paul at this point. Peter didn't have any money either. "Mom, I don't make enough money to cover my own bills, much less yours."

"Tom's happy to kick in." Constance dismissed Savannah with a cutesy wink and flick of her ring bejeweled hand. "He's a nice man. You might consider keeping him company at least. What would a date or two hurt? He likes you. Make him happy."

Savannah bit her lip. Her worst nightmare was for her security to depend on how happy she kept a man in bed. And that's what Mom was insinuating. "Tom has graciously offered to introduce me to some of his acquaintances. But I'll tell you the same thing I told him. Don't read more than friendship into this."

"Savannah, we don't need to have this conversation again, do we? Remember, it's easier to train a rich man to be sexy than to train a sexy one to be rich." Constance said with a teasing smile.

Savannah dismissed her mother's suggestion and fought for composure, poking the sprig of mint until it sank to the bottom of the glass. "I've been considering other solutions to our problem."

"Oh?" Constance said.

Courage. "If we cut back a little on our expenses and you looked for a job, it

126

would lessen the stress on us both."

"A job?" Constance crossed her legs and picked a speck of lint off her Prada suede ankle boot. Mom didn't have the money to pay her mortgage and she bought Pradas? "Honey, I invested all Daddy's life insurance in you and Chelsea's education to enable you to rub shoulders with the social elite of this city. What am I trained for? I've never worked a day in my life."

Except as an underage exotic dancer where she'd met Daddy. "What about a receptionist job?"

"Stop." Mom held out both hands. "I'm not trying to be difficult, but why would I take some menial position that won't come close to covering my expenses?"

"At least limit your expenses. Clean your own house." Savannah gritted her teeth at the tapping of Constance's acrylic nails on the wooden chair arm. "Cut out the manicures."

"Listen to yourself. That wouldn't add up to enough to pay my personal trainer."

Savannah set her glass on a gleaming silver coaster and tried to decide whether her mother was teasing or just totally out of touch with reality. Appearance was a driving factor with Mom. The one hope she saw at landing a rich husband and salvaging the life she'd worked so hard for. "Put the house on the market and move into an apartment then. Get your equity out to help you through while you figure

Partners By Design

out how to earn a living. What about real estate?"

Mom's green eyes teared. "Sell my house?"

"Mom, this isn't easy, but I don't see any other choice."

Constance stood and strode to the mantle, fingering a family photo taken a year or so before Daddy died. "This house is all I have left of your father. Our memories together. Our family. Our dreams."

What about my dreams? "I'm not going to date or marry a guy just because he has more money than Bill Gates."

Mom let out one of her infamous, long, exasperated sighs. "You are being unreasonable."

"Don't my feelings enter into this equation?"

Constance's voice softened. "Look, I loved your father. We had a good life together. He was the first person I ever met with a college degree. But a diploma doesn't come with a guarantee of financial success. Your daddy promised to take care of me, to buy me nice things. But look at me. I'm almost destitute. You may not understand now, but down the road you'll thank me."

"Think about what you're saying. I loved Logan more than I've ever loved anyone and he left me. You loved Daddy and he left you. Not by choice, granted, but the end result is the same. He's not here and you're on your own. Chelsea admitted that if she fought Jared on this move, she'd be out the door."

Her mother's eyes narrowed. "And your point is?"

"I want financial security."

"What's more secure than marrying well?"

"How can it be secure if I'm depending on another person to provide everything? What if he decides to take a hike like Donald did to you?" Savannah set her jaw. "The only security we have is to support ourselves."

Constance paced around the room, then took a seat on the sofa and clasped Savannah's hands. "Okay, we're in this together, as always. How about this?"

Wary of her mother's change of tactic, Savannah waited.

"I'll schedule the maid to only come once a month. And I'll do my own nails until we get on top of things. I'll cancel my plans to trade in the Caddie. But in return..."

Savannah let out her breath. "In return?"

"Give Tom a real chance. Consider all he has to offer." She squeezed Savannah's hands. "Sweetie, I've protected you from the seamier side of life. Having doors slammed in your face because you didn't know the right people or have the right clothes." Constance straightened Savannah's collar and arranged a lock of

Partners By Design

hair. "I know Logan broke your heart before. Remember, I'm the one who picked up the pieces. But that doesn't mean all men leave. Lust wanes in time. A tight pre-nup doesn't."

In her own unique way, Mom made a weird kind of sense. Logan had made promises before that he hadn't kept. And there was no logical reason why she shouldn't trust Tom. And Savannah could no longer afford not to be logical.

* * *

Savannah rushed by the office at lunch Monday and found Mallory at the reception desk pecking away on her laptop.

"Hi." Mallory jotted something in the notebook beside her, and then sat back. "I was turning into Bridezilla trying to plan a wedding in six weeks and work two jobs. So, I quit."

"Quit?"

"The day job. I was only planning to work another month anyway. Now I have time to help cover the phones, finish up our two contracts, and arrange the wedding without having to clock in. Quentin said he'd pitch in a few bucks if I needed him to."

That was one reprieve, even if short lived. "Any time you can spare would be great." Savannah straightened her jacket. "Aren't you going to ask why I have on a navy business suit?"

Mallory scratched her head. "It is a bit over-dressed for hanging mini-blinds."

"I spent the last two hours at the SBA, filling out forms for a small business loan."

"Okay. Does this mean Tom's out of the picture?"

"Tom promised to make some introductions, put in a few good words. I'm not going to base a romantic decision on finances." Savannah dropped her purse on the desk and studied her friend. "You're in love, right?"

"Oh yeah." Mallory beamed. "So?"

"How do you know? I mean, there has to be something, a specific moment."

"Well." She twisted a spike of hair. "I'm thinking that if you have to ask, it hasn't happened."

Oh, it had happened. "Why can't I just make my mother happy and fall in love with Tom, or someone like him?"

Mallory tilted her head in one of those do-I-have-to-spell-this-out looks. "I can think of at least one reason. One with super sexy jeans."

Savannah rolled her eyes, picturing Logan's tight little buns in jeans, or not.

"Oh." Mallory handed her a slip of paper. "This lady's called three times about a townhouse in Ridglea she just inherited. Said it needs a major facelift and Tom told her you were awesome."

Savannah fingered the paper and smiled. "He's doing what he promised."

Mallory shrugged. "Certainly can introduce your name into lucrative circles."

The truth was that starting a real relationship with Tom *could* provide not only a boost to her business, but protection. Emotional protection against falling back in love with Logan.

Which was the one thing that scared her more than financial destitution.

But no matter what Tom said, she still felt a little guilty dragging him into this, knowing she'd never love him.

Savannah turned as Logan entered. He glanced from one to the other and that funny little wrinkle appeared between his eyes. "What's going on?"

Mallory swiped two blue memos off the desk and held them out.

The furrow deepened as he took the messages. "I didn't expect anybody to be here today."

While Mallory explained her plan, Savannah avoided Logan's gaze. He didn't even acknowledge her before disappearing into his office. She waited by the desk a couple minutes until he returned, carrying a brown binder.

"Thanks, Mallory. Let me know if there is anything I can do to make this up to you. See you tomorrow."

Not so much as a hello or kiss my ass to Savannah on his way out the door. She turned to Mallory, but she'd developed a keen interest in the computer screen.

Partners By Design

"Goodbye, Logan!" Savannah spat and narrowed her eyes at her friend's quiet snicker.

This was ridiculous. She understood that he was angry or confused by her behavior, but he wasn't going to get away with ignoring her. They'd never be able to work together under these conditions. She whirled and took off after him. "Logan, wait up."

He stopped in front of the pickup, but didn't turn. "What?"

"We need to talk."

"Don't," he snapped.

She stepped in front of him. "Don't talk? Not talking about what happened after the fair won't make it go away."

"No. I'm not doing this." His expression matched his tone. "We both need this business arrangement to work. So before we screw it up any more than we already have, let's just focus on that. I'm late for an appointment."

She winced as the pickup door slammed and the engine revved. Could she work in the same office with him without venturing further down the illicit path? Would the sexual tension dissipate before it drove her over the brink of sanity?

She had to give Mom credit for knowing men. Probably the only shot Savannah had at getting Logan out of her system for good was to screw his brains out. Or would sex just cement her infatuation with her first lover?

133

Partners By Design

    Not that it mattered. Logan seemed to have gotten past his desire to find out.

    Fine. She grabbed her cell phone out of her pocket. If Logan didn't want to pursue their relationship, fine! Just...fine. Didn't matter. Neither did she. What she needed were some solid contracts.

Partners By Design

Chapter Eleven

    What was that sickening sweet smell? Logan slammed his truck door, rounded the corner of the office building and jerked back his fist before realizing the guy standing in front of a stack of hay bales was stuffed with straw. Pumpkins, scarecrows, and black cats? On the edge of the sidewalk a craggy witch stooped over a cast iron cauldron.

    Gregory didn't do this. The guy might own the building, but he didn't seem like the Halloween type.

    Illuminated only by the energy-saver evening lighting, the lobby hadn't escaped the eerie mystique either. Wispy webs crawling with hairy spiders swathed the balcony railings. Bats hung upside down from the eaves. Incandescent white ghosts soared across the lobby. Gregory must have hired a décor-a—. Savannah!

    He grabbed the banister and spun to defend himself as a cat shrieked a blood curdling "Yeowww!" The motion-activated beast perched on the bottom step ready to pounce, back arched, hair spiked along its spine, its tail whipping back and forth.

    Sucking air into his lungs and

stepping around it, Logan flinched at a second "Yeowww!"

He barged into the suite to find it strewn with orange and black decorations and Savannah laboring away like an elf in Santa's Halloween workshop.

"That possessed feline's gotta go."

She looked up and flashed a dimple. "Spooked, Mr. Reid?"

A stray tendril of hair escaped her ponytail and tickled her bare neck. Dammit. With everything else that needed his focus, Logan didn't want to deal with the 'Savannah desire' stress factor tonight. After teaching the design class, he'd left campus and delivered the proposal to his prospective client. All he wanted was to spend a couple hours putting the finishing tweaks on the drawing and then go home and crash.

Do not react to her. "Gregory hire you?"

"Not exactly." She stood and held up a blinking ceramic ghost. "This is for your office."

He nailed her with a glare.

She placed the ghost on the corner of the receptionist desk. "Don't scowl at me. I talked him into paying for materials, but I'm donating my time for promotion. This is going to save us."

"You giving away free labor is going to save us?"

He didn't like the implication of

Partners By Design

that sexy little twinkle. Being around her was more of a challenge with each passing day. He hated the intense attraction. It was a lost cause. They had no future, yet she could draw him in with a simple grin. Hell, it didn't even take that. Even pissed off, she wound him up.

"When you're starting out in a new location, you have to let people know you're here. Generate interest. I talked to the other businesses. We're all decorating our offices and stocking up on candy for the kids." She tucked a strand of hair behind her ear and a diamond stud winked at him. "I'm in charge of advertising."

"And these kids are going to hire us to build and decorate their playhouses? I get all the trading cards. You can keep the Monopoly money?"

Her lips tightened. "We list all our businesses and contact info on the flyers. We hand out little sacks of candy and staple our business cards to them. We stack extra cards by the door. Have them fill out cards for a drawing so we collect names and phone numbers. Can you think of a better way to draw people in to see what we're all about?"

"I never got into Halloween."

"I'm dressing like a gypsy and reading palms."

Savannah in some sexy gypsy outfit! Oh yeah, his stress factor just quadrupled!

"And you and Mallory dress up as

fellow gypsies and wave people in. Hand out candy and chat up the parents while I tell the kid's fortunes." She tossed a red scarf over her arm and held a blousy white shirt against his shoulders. "This should fit."

"All the other businesses bought into this?"

"They love it. Mr. Gregory got so excited, he wouldn't stop talking." She flashed another enigmatic grin. The realtors are going to decorate and run the haunted house."

"Haunted house?"

"It won't take much for you to build one for the lobby, right?"

His jaw tightened. "And when am I going to find time to do this between now and the weekend?"

"Don't worry about anything except building it. Well, and the tent. The lawyer downstairs has a tent for my palm reading, if you can figure out how to put it up without stakes."

Don't worry about anything except the haunted house. Right? And don't forget to dress in an asinine costume and chat up the visitors. And then there's this tent to set up all without damaging a polished wood floor.

"I assured him you were the man for the job, no sweat." Her laughter followed as she shoved him toward his office. "Mr. Gregory is going to be Herman Munster. And his wife has a witch costume and she'll hand out candy from the caldron, with dry ice for smoke and everything. Don't you just love it?"

Savannah vibrated with the anticipation of a kid at Disneyland. She was steam-rolling him, but he had no idea how to get out of this lunacy without looking like an ass.

"Gregory gets to be Herman Munster while I'm stuck wearing a pansy shirt?" He frowned. "Something's wrong here."

* * *

How the hell had she suckered him into building a haunted house? He needed one of those 'Just Say No' T-shirts from high school. He'd been addicted from his first taste of Savannah Holt years before. And the thought of her dressed as a gypsy was more dangerous than any damn barbiturate.

Logan was coming out of the kitchen with his first cup of coffee the next morning when Savannah blew into the office like fall foliage in brown slacks and an orange and yellow sweater. She ran her fingers through her windblown hair as he sipped the steaming coffee and took in the view.

"You're here a lot more lately," she said.

Keep it professional. Don't picture her naked. "Yeah, I wrapped up one project. Only a couple more jobs to finish and I'm independent. No more slaving for the man." He leaned against the door. "Of course, that also means no more regular paycheck. What are you doing here?"

"Argh. A mandatory day off. With all the time I've taken for this business, I'm on my boss's shit list. When I asked for another long lunch, he suggested I take the whole day and figure out whether I want to be employed by Windows To Go or not."

"Not good."

"As bad as I want to be on my own, I'm sunk without a steady paycheck." She tossed her purse on the desk and dropped into the chair, massaging her temples. "Finished, over, kaput."

One look at the drooping corners of her pouty lips and he caved. It wasn't his place to solve her problems, but he could at least take her mind off them for an hour. "Remember that Tudor design you helped me with the other night?" He held up the key. "I got the contract. Want to take a look?"

"Wow! Congratulations." Savannah slung her purse over her shoulder and grinned. "Race you to the truck."

* * *

Cars lined both sides of the street as Logan wedged the truck between a Mercedes and a Volkswagen crowding the road.

Beautiful day. Still early and crisp. Breezy enough to shower the neighborhood in fall leaves. Majestic oaks were one of the TCU trademarks.

She sighed. "Remember driving me

Partners By Design

through here when we were dating? I'd never heard anyone get so turned on about architecture. It was cool."

Evidently those two weeks in high school had changed both their lives in ways he'd never considered.

Savannah held her hair back from blowing in her face and pointed across the street. "An estate sale. Do we have time?"

Given the way her day was going, he didn't have the heart to say no, even if he had more work at the office than he could get done. "Thirty minutes."

All the nice pieces were pricey. Savannah crouched and ran her hand over a small cabinet with rows of narrow drawers. "Isn't it beautiful?" She twisted the big red 'Sold' tag. "I've been looking for a spool cabinet, but the ones I can afford are always sold."

He bent to check out the solid walnut frame and glass front drawers. A few scratches and scuffmarks, just enough to add character. "And you'd use it for what?"

"For my sewing and upholstery supplies." She opened a narrow drawer and picked a tiny black thread off the pink felt. "Dressmakers and shops used them to hold spools of thread."

She ran one hand over the surface before continuing to browse through the house. "You can't find things like this anymore. Mom thinks it's all junk."

Even if her mother didn't like

141

antiques, wouldn't she at least notice how much Savannah loved them? "I'm sure you can find a spool cabinet."

"And pay for it how? I'm on the verge of unemployment." She weighed the shape of a red crystal water goblet then replaced it in the set and headed back across the street empty-handed.

Although Savannah seemed to appreciate his plans to renovate the Tudor, she acted fidgety walking through the house, preoccupied. Her mood today proved how strapped for cash she was.

"Do you think this house is haunted?" she asked, pulling him out of his musings.

"Haunted? As in ghosts?" He couldn't keep from grinning. "Haven't run up against any."

Shrugging, she opened the hall closet and poked around like she expected to find a friendly spook perched on the shelf with the dust bunnies. "You never know about these old places."

Logan couldn't decide whether it was quirkier that she believed in ghosts or that she didn't seem frightened of them. Knowing Savannah, she'd round them all up and invite them to the damn Halloween shindig.

He followed her down the hall, wondering how she'd react to the small rock fireplace in the master.

As expected, that was the first thing she focused on. "Oh man, can you imagine snuggling up in here on a cold winter

Partners By Design

night with a good book?"

"A book wasn't my first thought," he said before thinking.

She didn't even blush, just flashed him a cutesy smile and drifted back to the kitchen. He could see her mentally jotting down notes as she stood on the faded linoleum and turned. "This is a dream job. Wonder if they're interested in hiring a decorator. I even have a couple landscape design courses under my belt."

"I'll let them know." He unlocked the backdoor for her to check out the overgrown yard while he ambled back to the front window. An older gentleman was loading the spool cabinet into the trunk of a Mercedes.

The way Savannah had looked at that cabinet tugged at his heart. Almost erotic how she'd caressed the smooth wood. Savannah made the most menial tasks look sexual. Hell, he'd watched mesmerized as she loaded orange paper into the copier last night.

He hurried down the drive and handed the guy his business card. "My friend has her heart set on that spool cabinet. Wouldn't make me a deal, would you?"

Co-workers bought each other gifts, right?

* * *

Logan rolled out artificial turf to protect the hardwood floor in the lobby then pulled his jacket on. Temperature had plummeted as dusk fell and the smell of rain hung in the air, but according to the weather report, it'd move out before tomorrow night's festivities.

Thunder rumbled and rain pelted the sidewalk as one of the lawyers helped him haul the last load of lumber in. Logan laid it on the floor, shoved his hood off, and skimmed the water from his arms.

Did Savannah have a clue what she'd started or how much work she'd generated with this half-baked idea? Everyone seemed to have a task and the offices resembled a Halloween carnival more than places of business.

A couple of the guys pitched in to help construct the haunted house frame. The realtors planned to do the rest with black plastic and a staple gun.

Savannah lugged an army green duffel out of the lawyer's office. "Here's the tent. Need any help?" she asked, dropping the duffel by the wall. "I can at least hold boards in place."

"We've got it," Logan said.

She flashed one of those thousand watt smiles guaranteed to have any red-blooded male sniffing at her heals like a stray puppy. "Since everyone is working tonight, Mr. Gregory is springing for pizza. I volunteered to make a beer run. Any special orders?"

"If it's beer, I'll drink it," the preppy lawyer said, returning the smile with a little too much enthusiasm for Logan's comfort.

"You're easy." Savannah flashed the lawyer her megawatt smile.

She'd been out to dinner the past two evenings with the Lexus jerk, yet every time Logan turned around she invaded his space. As if he and Truesdale weren't enough, now she proceeded to flirt with this poor, unsuspecting lawyer.

The evening turned into a decorating extravaganza with Savannah the ringleader of the chaos. She mingled with the other tenants like she'd known them all her life. As she worked the room, Logan marveled at how she always ended up the center of attention.

The lawyer sat on the floor beside Logan and swallowed a mouthful of pepperoni pizza. "She's a doll."

Logan slugged his beer and ignored the comment, but his gaze followed the lawyer's. As if sensing his stare, Savannah turned from her perch on the bottom stair and flashed a half grin. Excusing herself from the realtor, she chatted her way through the crowd, grabbed a slice of pizza, and joined them on the floor. Logan didn't miss that she sat by the lawyer and not him.

She swallowed a bite. "The place is looking great! Hope the weather clears and we have a good turnout."

"It'll move out before noon," the lawyer promised, squeezing her hand.

"This thing isn't going to build itself." Logan nudged the attorney's shoulder before the guy became Savannah's

Partners By Design

next victim.

Savannah stood and dusted off the seat of her jeans. "Well, it sounds like you two have this under control. Guess I'll get started on our suite."

Logan finished securing the frame and headed upstairs to throw together a platform for Savannah's gypsy tent. An orange and brown wreath of leaves hung on the suite door. Inside, a giant cornucopia engulfed the receptionist desk. "Where did that thing come from?"

Savannah tied a black ribbon on an orange cellophane bag of candy corn and glanced at the massive arrangement.

"Tom sent it for luck."

Figured. He grabbed the sheet of plywood he'd bought to bolt the tent to. "Where do you want this?"

"In the center of my office." She followed him into the room. "I moved the desks."

He tried to ignore the ribbon of skin above her tight, low-cut jeans and concentrate on measuring the width of the room. If he could just focus he'd be done in an hour and out of here. And away from her.

"Can I do anything to help?" she asked, straightening and bumping into Logan in the process. She ran her palms down her jeans and avoided his eyes.

"Nothing," he snapped.

* * *

Savannah called Logan's cell phone for the second time. "Are you on the way? It's almost dark."

"Exiting off I-30."

"Call me when you get close." Tonight had her psyched. Not only was it going to be fun, but with a little luck they'd score at least a couple leads.

Five minutes later, her cell phone chimed, "<u>I Love a Rainy Night</u>."

"I'm pulling into the parking lot," Logan said.

"Rush it up. You still have to dress." She hung up and checked the office to make sure they hadn't missed any last minute details. She had cups and orange punch and black cat shaped Halloween cookies. Plastic glasses and chilled wine for the adults along with info cards to fill out for a drawing to win a free consultation. The Gregorys were already stationed out front to flag in the crowds.

As soon as Logan came through the door, she took his laptop and shoved his costume into his hands. "Hurry."

He didn't move, just stared at her chest.

She glanced at the off-shoulder blouse and felt a flush all the way to her exposed cleavage.

"You look," He blinked. "Like a gypsy."

Mallory strolled into the room and followed the line of Logan's gaze. Mallory

Partners By Design

sing-songed the lyrics of <u>I Love a Rainy Night</u> as she bustled past.

Savannah glared at Mallory's back and gave Logan a push toward the restroom. "Get dressed." The warmth of his gaze lingered even after he'd gone to change.

He was back out in a flash, messing with the full shirtsleeves. "How are you supposed to wear this thing?"

Oh, wow. "Here, let me help." She tugged the shirt loose from his pants a little to give it volume, then buttoned the cuffs and poofed out the sleeves, trying to ignore his tight biceps. Helping him dress felt too intimate, too much like they were a couple. She took a step back. "Looks good. Where's the bandana?"

Logan pulled it from his pocket and held it out. She tied it around his dark blond hair and clipped a small hoop on his right ear.

He grabbed her hand. "Hey, I don't wear earrings."

"Logan the architect doesn't, but Logan the gypsy does. Deal with it." Needing something to busy her hands, she retrieved a tambourine off the desk. "Here. Just dance around and make noise. Draw attention."

"What?" He frowned at the tambourine as if he'd never seen one.

She swayed her hips, tapping the tambourine against her hand. "Come if you dare. Have dazzling gypsy Savannah read your palm and reveal the future."

"You've already got me poured into pants that are a size too small. I'm wearing a damn earring and a girl's shirt. Now you want me to wiggle my ass and play a tambourine?" He leaned toward her. "You're pushing your luck, Gypsy Savannah."

She danced back and forth. "Come on, Logan. I know you can move."

Before she could react, he yanked her hard against his body. Savannah wasn't sure whether the fire behind the navy eyes was passion or anger. She shook her hair over her shoulders and grasped his arms, trying to maintain an inch of decorum. His hips moved intimately with hers and her cheeks heated.

Her softness molded against Logan's hardness down to her curling toes. She moistened her lips and her mouth hungered for his.

As children's laughter filled the lobby below, Logan eased Savannah away. "Stop playing with me. If you're bored with Truesdale, buy a damn toy."

She shoved his chest and escaped to her tent to hide her frustration. *Just deal with the business tonight.* Her unrelenting draw to Logan...well she'd figure that out tomorrow.

* * *

Savannah's skin prickled with excitement as the building filled with tiny superheroes, goblins, and fairy princesses. Now if some of their parents would require the services of either an architect or an interior designer.

Gypsies Logan and Mallory worked the outer office, talking with clients, serving refreshments and passing out candy bags. Savannah read so many palms she exhausted the list of responses, but the kids ate it up. Even some of the adults requested her services.

Every so often Mallory would shake the tambourine to the tune of, "I love a rainy night," throwing in the random lyric. Hopefully, Logan had never heard the ring-tone she'd selected for him. He'd never recognize the old Eddie Rabbit song, at least not if Mallory would give it a rest.

Mallory's fiancé, Quentin, strolled in a little before nine. Some bleached blonde in screw-my-brains-out black leather pants and a jungle print blouse had been talking to Logan for at least half an hour. She even had felt cat ears stuck to a headband. Savannah read both her children's fortunes, but the woman lingered in the reception area long after they'd tromped off to the other offices. Savannah tilted her head for a closer look as the urban cougar ran a manicured claw over Logan's arm. One of them better at least get a contract.

The trick-or-treaters were beginning to thin out and only a few straggling kids were squealing through the haunted house. Savannah stood and rolled her head to alleviate the stiffness. She'd been sitting hunched over for three hours.

Logan returned from walking the

blonde out and swiped the bandana off his head. "We got a couple leads."

She hid a grin watching him struggle not to stare at her cleavage. "As long as we get even one contract, tonight was worth it. Did Mallory leave?"

He brought his gaze back to her face. "She and Quentin couldn't keep their hands off each other. I told them to shove off before the gremlins got a dose of sex education."

"Considerate of you."

She looked at the dark circles under his eyes. He'd been a good sport to put up with her plan even though he didn't have time. And he'd been diligent in working the crowd.

He ran his hands through his sweaty hair, pushing it out of his face. "You were right. Tonight worked."

"Coming from you, I'll take that as a compliment."

"Sounds like the trick-or-treaters are winding down." He glanced into the almost empty candy bowl. "Good thing."

"Yes, it is." Savannah worried her bottom lip. Logan was one of those guys who looked best a bit tousled and tonight he epitomized the perfect specimen. Tight black jeans, blousy white shirt, and finger tracks in his spikey hair. Jealousy still burning from the blonde's acute interest in him, Savannah reached out and took his hand. "Come into my tent, Gypsy Logan. Let's explore whether the lady in the leather pants is going to pay off."

"As long as I get to sit." Logan looked exhausted, but followed her into her candle-lit tent. He dropped cross-legged onto the hot pink and orange cushion across from her and placed his hand in her outstretched palm. "You don't believe this stuff, right?"

Her thumb skimmed the calluses on his fingertips. "A smart man never questions a gypsy's psychic powers." She ran both thumbs across his large palm and held it flat, recalling the pleasure that hand could evoke. "Long life line. This deep line is passion," she told him, scraping the tip of her fingernail down the crease. "And this one, the love line. Long with only one crack in the early part of your life. Was he actually capable of a long-lasting relationship?

Their eyes met and she fought to keep her pulse from racing. God, he looked incredible.

Logan shook his head. "So all this work to generate contracts. The success of this business seems like life and death to you."

She accepted the change of subject. "I have to be self-sufficient. I will never rely on any man to support me. Even my dad left."

Logan's eyes narrowed. "You should be able to support yourself. But your father died. Don't think that was his choice. And neither is it fair to toss us all in the same bucket. Not all men walk away."

"You did!" she snapped before engaging her brain.

He gulped and his mouth moved, but the word seemed delayed. "Savannah." He paused as if waiting on his thoughts to catch up. "If it helps, the circumstances were out of my control."

Tears threatened. She shook her head in confusion. "The age difference thing?"

One dark eyebrow cocked. "I shouldn't have..."

She waited, hoping he'd elaborate, make sense. He flexed his fingers as if trying to keep them from fisting.

"God I loved you, Savannah."

The lump in her throat constrained her breathing and her eyes watered. She watched the soft candlelight glint off his hair and dance across his face. Mesmerizing her, pulling her under his spell.

Slowly, she brought his hand up and kissed his palm, watching his face. She nipped his pinky finger with her teeth.

The corner of his mouth twitched in that sexy sideways grin as he ran his finger along the inside of her bottom lip. Her heart exploded with liquid heat.

This was her Logan. The boy who'd taken her on the most exciting, passion-filled two weeks any girl could dream of.

And tenderness.

Their eyes locked. She'd loved him more than life itself. And he'd loved her.

There was nothing for him to gain by lying about the past now.

"Thanks for telling me that." Rising on her knees, she leaned across the table and touched her lips to his.

"Come here." Taking her hand, he pulled her around the table and into his lap. His hand tangled in her hair. His tongue traced her lips then began an age old duel with hers as he eased her down onto the soft cushion.

Instinctively she spread her legs and allowed Logan to settle in between. His jean covered erection pressed against her damp softness.

Logan kissed his way around her chin and down her neck, lowering the elastic neckline of her peasant blouse and kissing the mole on her right breast. She sighed. That little mole had always fascinated him. He pushed her strapless bra down and sucked her nipple into his mouth. Arching her back, she gave him full access, wanting more. Wanting all of Logan.

His other hand scrunched her skirt up and grasped the back of her thigh, spreading her legs wider then slid beneath the leg of her panties. He slipped a finger inside her wetness and started to pump.

"Savannah." Tom's distant voice penetrated her euphoric haze. She hadn't expected him to actually show up.

The air crackled in the dim, candle lit tent as Logan pulled back. She held a finger to his lips, lips still glistening

Partners By Design

with her kiss. "Shh." Maybe if they were quiet Tom would disappear.

Chapter Twelve

Logan yanked his blousy shirt out of his jeans and let it fall loosely before ducking out of the tent. Savannah squelched her lust and pulled her bra and blouse back into place, watching Logan's departing backside.

"Hey, Tom," Logan said.

She blew out the candle and tried to still her shaking hands. Her stomach rolled, as if she'd consumed too much Halloween candy.

The artificial reception area light seemed harsh in comparison to the dim lit tent. As she stepped out, Tom zeroed in on her low cut peasant blouse. Was she turning into her mother? Not that she'd chosen this outfit for Logan, or had she? Then after that cougar, she'd definitely set out to capture his attention, craved it. Pure green-eyed jealousy.

Both eyebrows rose as Tom stared from her to Logan and back, then flashed a composed grin. "How was the turnout?"

Picking up the candy bowl, Savannah sorted through the contents. "We only have seven bags left out of two hundred and fifty."

"I ate two of those, by the way."

Partners By Design

Logan jabbed his fingers through his hair. "But we made some good contacts, thanks to Savannah's ingenious plan."

Tom seemed transfixed on her cleavage. "She's a smart businesswoman."

A tiny red devil and an angelic mermaid trounced into the office with their mom close on their heels.

Logan dropped a bag of candy into each of their plastic pumpkins.

"How about a cookie and punch?" Savannah offered.

The mother let them each select a cookie from the platter before they raced out the door toward the next office in their last minute quest for loot.

Tom watched them leave, and then smiled at Savannah. "Hoped to entice you into joining me for dinner."

She turned off the blinking ghost. After her interlude with Logan, she wasn't up to dinner with Tom or anyone. "I have to clean up."

"I'm sure you're exhausted. It'll wait until morning." Tom poked a bale of hay with the toe of his dress shoe.

"Logan and I can clean this in nothing flat before we leave. I have mounds of work tomorrow." She transferred the remaining cookies into the plastic container Mallory had brought them in. All she could think about was getting home and savoring what Logan had said about having been in love with her.

Partners By Design

"Tomorrow is Sunday, Savannah." Tom glanced up as Logan came out of the kitchen with a black trash bag.

Savannah gathered up discarded orange plastic cups and stacked them together. "Tom, I do appreciate the offer, but it's been a really long day." She tossed the sticky cups into Logan's bag, with an appreciative grin.

Tom stood in the center of the reception area, as if he wasn't sure what had changed in the game.

Neither was Savannah.

Tom lifted an empty wine bottle off the desk and studied the label. "Guess I'll head out," he said, setting it back on the desk with a clunk.

"I appreciate you stopping by." Savannah waited until the front door closed before ambling out to the hall to lean over the railing.

Mr. Gregory escorted the last trick-or-treaters out the front door. He looked up and applauded. "Savannah, splendid evening."

"It was, wasn't it?" she said, flashing him a grin.

Gregory waved toward the door. "You two shove off. We're all leaving. Tomorrow is soon enough to put this place back in shape."

Savannah gestured him away. "You go on. I'll lock up."

Logan turned just as she stooped to

peel a glob of sticky candy off the wood floor. Too late, she realized that from his height, he had a view all the way to her belly button.

"He's right. We can finish this tomorrow," Logan said, diverting his eyes.

She flinched and straightened at his clipped tone. "I'll just pick up a little."

"Get out of here, Savannah!" He blew out a breath and his voice softened. "Please."

* * *

When Savannah arrived to clean Sunday morning, the realtor on the first floor met her at the door, stuffing black and orange crepe paper into a trash bag. "I lined up two listings last night!"

"We drew a good crowd." Savannah glanced around the lobby, but a pile of decorations against the wall was the only sign of the haunted house. "I planned to help tear everything down."

The realtor shrugged. "The haunted house was gone when we arrived an hour ago. Figured you and Logan disassembled it last night."

"Not me," Savannah said, heading upstairs. Except for a similar neat crate of decorations beside her door, hard to tell there'd even been a party in their suite.

Logan had sent her home last night and done all this himself.

Frustration?

She could relate.

As she opened her office door, her gaze landed on a small wooden cabinet in the corner. The spool cabinet from the estate sale. Reverently, she trailed her fingers over the hand-worn wood and read her name on a pastel yellow envelope.

She slid one finger beneath the flap and removed a simple card with a picture of an old stone house surrounded by country clutter. A rocking chair sat on the weathered porch where a straw hat and a pair of dirty garden slippers waited for their owner to return.

Inside the card he'd written. 'Enjoy it, Logan.'

Tears filled her eyes. Her hand trembled as she re-read the card. How had he pulled this off? And why?

She couldn't concentrate as she hauled the decorations to the van and put her office back together. While she waited for Logan to arrive, she kept getting up to touch and admire the spool cabinet. She wasn't sure if she loved the cabinet itself or the idea of the gift most. She wasn't sure about much of anything when it came to Logan Reid.

By noon, she gave up and dialed Logan's cell phone. When it rolled to voice mail, she hung up. This thanks warranted more than a voicemail.

* * *

"I need to see who's on the other

line." Logan shifted his truck into Park. Kat wasn't giving up today. He didn't have time to spend every Sunday at the lake.

"Fine. I'll tell Nathan not to count on you for lunch, again today. Tell Savannah the shutters look great." Kat clicked off.

Logan shouldered his laptop and entered the lobby, pushing redial on Savannah's cell number. As he opened the suite door, he heard her phone. He was so exhausted, he hadn't even noticed her van in the parking lot. What was that tune? It sounded familiar, but the title eluded him. "Hey."

Savannah was sitting at her desk when he walked into her office. "Hey," she said into the phone, then looked up and flipped her phone shut.

He hung up as she came across the office and brushed her lips across his cheek. "Thank you for the spool cabinet. I can't believe you did that."

Her breasts pressed against his chest. Intense electrical sparks ignited and blazed through his body. He gritted his teeth and took a step back.

Savannah backed away as well, eyes wide, and ran her palms down her slacks.

"You're welcome. I just thought..." He wasn't sure what he'd thought. He fumbled for a neutral topic. "By the way, I talked to the guy about you bidding on that kitchen redesign. He said to bring it on. If it's not too high, he'd consider it."

Partners By Design

"Thank you!" She took a deep breath and offered a tentative grin. "Do you mind checking the bid when I'm done and making sure I'm in line?"

"Sure. But I promised him you'd have it to him by Wednesday." Crap. His voice sounded as shaky as hers. He escaped to his office, but her innocent kiss had short-circuited his brain. They either had to hook up or end this working arrangement. The torture was going to do him in.

And he couldn't place that stupid tune from her cell phone. Mom was <u>You and Me Against the World</u>. Most calls were <u>Don't Worry Be Happy</u>. The ringtone for his number wasn't either one.

* * *

Logan heard high heels clicking across the floor, but he still flinched as his office door banged against the wall Monday morning. "Ms. Holt," he said, pushing back his chair and standing.

Constance's glare made his skin crawl as she scaled him down to his boots. "Who the hell do you think you are ruining my daughter's life, again?

Hold your ground. "Her life. Her choice. Nothing to do with you."

"I won't stand by and watch her flush her future down the toilet now anymore than I did the first time around."

He squared his shoulders and fought the sick memories of his past with this woman. "Don't threaten me, Ms. Holt."

She waved a pearl white cell phone. "Don't push me, Mr. Reid. One call and I can destroy any chance you think you have for a relationship with Savannah."

What made her think there was anything to destroy? "And ruin your own relationship with her in the process," he added.

Ignoring his remark, she marched across the room and got in his face. "What do you have to offer her? Tom Truesdale owns his own business. A nice home. A company jet. His family has millions. He could give Savannah the world."

"His world. Truesdale doesn't even know what Savannah wants."

She took a dainty step back. Diamonds sparkled and silver bracelets clinked as she ran her hands over her flat stomach and made a production of smoothing her skintight white blouse. "Savannah would never have to worry about money again."

"Nor would you. You have any qualms about selling your daughter to the highest bidder?"

Sparks of intense hatred shot from her eyes. "End it or I will." She turned on her four-inch heels and strutted from the office, leaving the door open in her wake.

"Bitch!" Logan grabbed a Nerf ball off the desk and threw it as hard as he could at the wall. It hit silently and fell to the floor. His heart rate slowly steadied.

Desperate or not, he had no sympathy for a woman who would stoop so low to manipulate her daughter. How did she justify thinking that Savannah was obligated to provide her a living? A high end living at that.

A realization slowly penetrated his anger. No matter whether Truesdale was in the picture or not, Constance Holt believed her daughter's feelings for Logan presented a threat. Even if it wasn't true, it provided a measure of satisfaction that Constance thought so.

But his temporary vindication was squelched by the knowledge of how Savannah would be destroyed if the truth came out.

* * *

Savannah was more comfortable with Logan than with any man since her father died. And more uncomfortable. She knew he was confused by this thing between them, but so was she. Her heart and mind were waging a battle for control.

Something had to change with her mother's situation. Donald was history and landing another sugar daddy wasn't the answer. Mom's relationships were getting shorter in duration and the times in between were stretching longer. There had to be another way.

If Savannah's design business didn't improve, all was going down the tube. The last thing she needed was the distraction of Logan. She couldn't survive him again if things went south. Yet she yearned to explore whether there was any possibility of a future there.

He'd admitted that he'd been in love with her.

The big question was could she trust him? There was more to their first breakup than age and a legal threat of statutory rape.

Tuesday, Logan's pickup was in the parking lot after work, yet he stayed hidden behind his closed office door, as he'd done the past two days.

Mallory had taken off early for an appointment with a lady who custom-made wedding veils. The quiet, calm office closed in on Savannah.

She called the design showroom to arrange a time to take her client to look at fabric and paint samples she'd chosen for the sun porch. Then spent an hour on the kitchen redesign bid.

If her luck held, Logan would leave for class and she wouldn't run into him before she left to meet Mom and the Truesdales for dinner. Bridgette Truesdale was still considering the bids.

Savannah went to the restroom and changed into a rust colored satin camisole and blazer. She touched up her makeup and sprayed a hint of Happy behind each ear.

Burning the candle at both ends, she kept more clothes here than at home. It saved her at least a half hour plus gas not to race home to change.

She locked her office and made her way to her van. With the shift from

Partners By Design

Daylight Savings Time, the sun had already set. The evening breeze blew cool and crisp. The transition from summer to fall was her favorite time of year. Pulling out all the richer, heavier fall fabrics and packing away the summer clothes equated to a new wardrobe without the expense.

Pitching her purse onto the floorboard, she fastened her seat belt and turned the key. Click, click, click.

She turned off the ignition, waited a few seconds, pumped the gas, and tried again. Same response. Great. She rested her forehead against the steering wheel. Just one more bill she couldn't afford. And Mom would start up again about buying a car. The last thing she wanted was an expensive car payment.

A quick tap on the window made her clutch her chest to restart her heartbeat.

"Problem?" Logan asked when she lowered the window.

"It just clicks."

He listened while she turned the key. "Pop the hood."

She pulled the lever. "Don't you have class tonight?"

"I gave them a free night to finish their projects for Thursday." After retrieving his tools from the truck, he had her turn the key again. "How old is your battery?"

"I replaced it last Christmas."

"It's probably the alternator then."

Partners By Design

"What's that going to run me?"

Logan pushed up his sleeves and pulled a screwdriver from his tool bag. "Not much."

She slid out of the van and stared at the seat of his slacks as he leaned under the hood. He held up a small box-shaped thingy with wires. "I'll run and pick up another one."

Savannah wasn't accustomed to men who repaired things themselves. "Are you sure you have time?"

"It's a quick job."

She followed him to the truck, hiked her tight skirt, and climbed in beside him. "I'll have to put the part on a credit card."

She checked her watch while he bought the part. She had about half an hour to get to the restaurant. She thought about calling and asking Tom to swing by and pick her up, but she didn't want to give him any ideas that she might be interested in more than a friendship. No matter what happened with Logan, Tom was not her future.

On the way back from the parts store, her cell phone rang. "We're at the restaurant," Mom said.

"I won't be long."

"What's the hold up? You were supposed to have a table and order hors d'oeuvres."

"Mom, the van won't start, but I'll

be there soon."

"This is ridiculous. I'll call you a cab," she said.

"Maybe you should go ahead without me tonight."

"This is your career," Mom reminded her.

"Pardon me for having car trouble," she said with a touch more edge than intended.

Logan pulled into the parking lot and got out. "Take the truck. By the time you finish dinner, the van should be running."

Her mouth fell open. "I can't leave you stranded without a vehicle." Mom was still grumbling in her ear. "Just a minute," she said into the phone, then put her hand over the mouthpiece. "Are you sure you don't mind?"

"No problem. I'll install the part and drive the van to the deli to grab a bite. Put a charge back in the battery. I'm going to be here until all hours tonight anyway."

"Mom, I'm on my way." She clicked off and glanced at the manual shifter.

Logan leaned in. "You can drive a stick. This one's just on the column. Here, let me show you the pattern."

She slid over, pressed the clutch and moved the shifter through the gears as Logan instructed. Of course she could drive a stick shift. He'd taught her the night they met. A game of strip driving had put a whole new spin on mastering a standard transmission.

"So if I bring it back in one piece, are you going to take your shirt off?" she asked then realized she'd spoken her thought aloud.

At first he looked stunned, then cocked an eyebrow. "Sure. But this time around you know how to drive a stick. Kill it and I want more than a damn kiss."

She felt her face heat at the sexy memories, but it was too late to recall her taunt. She dropped her van keys into his hand. "I appreciate this."

Logan shut the door and stood on the sidewalk, watching as she started the truck and backed up. She was half tempted to scratch first gear and see how he reacted.

She eased in the clutch and shifted into first gear. The truck jerked and rumbled out of the lot. Her mouth watered at the memory of that exquisite mixture of fear and excitement when she'd killed the Miata and the reality that Logan was going to kiss her.

Before she faced her dinner companions, she had to shake the erotic thoughts of that long ago night. But her traitorous body was in over-drive reliving the excitement of racing around a vacant parking lot with the sexiest bad boy she'd ever met and fantasizing about what might happen before the night ended.

A guy crazy enough to yank a black tee-shirt over his head for a girl on her sixteenth birthday just because she made it all the way around the parking lot without stalling the little car.

Concentrate, Savannah. Just forget him. Right. Forget the most passionate sixteen days, and nights, of her life.

Remember, he also dumped you without an explanation.

The restaurant was only a few miles. She accelerated through a yellow light and turned onto the expressway.

The pickup was wider and longer than her minivan and she had to back up twice to maneuver it into the narrow restaurant parking space. She turned off the engine and pulled the visor down. Half an hour late. Fresh lipstick couldn't hurt.

She'd never quite mastered the art of putting lipstick on without at least one smear. Digging in her purse, she didn't find a single tissue, not even a wadded up one. Popping the glove box open, she hoped for a napkin or something to blot the coppery smudge off the corner of her mouth.

A bra? A hairclip? She looked closer. Her bra and her hairclip. And a white plastic drug store bag containing a box of condoms. She read the receipt. He'd bought three boxes, the morning after the State Fair. The morning after that stormy night in his truck.

She pressed her legs together to squelch the longing. That night of the fair haunted her. Every time she even brushed against Logan, her hormones raged into an adolescent frenzy. She clutched the bag in her lap. "Oh, Logan. What am I going to do about you?"

Opening her eyes, she blinked at Mom sprinting down the sidewalk toward the truck. Savannah dabbed the lipstick with her pinky finger, wiped it on the bra, and shoved everything back inside the compartment.

Mom opened her door just as Savannah slammed the glove box. "Logan's truck, I presume?"

Savannah fought her temper. "How did you think I was going to get here?" She slid out and pressed the lock button.

"That's it. We have to get you a car. I've got other things to worry about rather than your safety."

And what did she plan to use for money? Savannah shook her head. "It was just the alternator and it's probably already running."

"We can find something. Tom made me a personal loan. We're good."

"What?" Savannah's stomach lurched and threatened to toss the dinner she hadn't yet eaten. "Did you ask him for money? How much?"

"He offered." Mom smiled. "Just enough to get us through."

"How much?" Savannah demanded.

"Just ten thousand. Help catch up the house and car payments and tide me over," Mom said starting toward the entrance.

Partners By Design

Savannah stopped dead. One more financial nail in her coffin. "You're giving it back."

"I don't have the money to give back. I paid my bills." Mom turned and gritted her teeth. "Grow up, Savannah. Time to take off your rose colored, I-can-do-it-myself, glasses and focus on cold, hard reality."

Chapter Thirteen

Savannah stared at the mock-up of Mrs. Campessi's new sunroom, but she didn't like the way the colors mixed. The rich reds and golds and dark woods were what the woman had requested, but they killed the open, airy room. Maybe she'd work up a second layout just for fun. Something brighter, sunnier.

She pushed back from her computer. Nothing pleased her today. She still couldn't believe her mother had accepted a loan from Tom. But as desperate as Mom was for money, she was even more desperate that Savannah pursue Tom. As much as Savannah didn't want to believe the worst of her mom, she suspected her mom accepted Tom's money just so Savannah would feel obligated.

And Logan had Savannah's bra in his glove box.

She squeezed her eyes closed and twisted her hair.

And he'd bought condoms.

The door clicked shut in the outer office, but it was after five and Mallory would take care of whoever it was. Savannah could do without any more issues today.

Partners By Design

    She listened, but she didn't hear her friend's cheery voice greeting their guest. Crap! Mallory had left fifteen minutes ago to meet the florist. She jumped up to deal with the visitor and met Logan in the reception area.

    Her eyes absorbed every inch of him. Every exhausted inch. The guy looked done in. "Thanks again for coming to my rescue last night."

    "You're welcome."

    She grinned. "Not sure what I'd have done if you hadn't still been here."

    "Ehh, you'd have called a garage." He winked. "You're not helpless."

    She felt warm all the way down to her toes. At least he realized she didn't have to be taken care of. She blew out her breath. "How about I spring for a pizza and beer as a token of thanks?"

    He looked as if he might argue, but changed his mind. "Fair enough. But, we have to hustle. I've got a long evening ahead framing the wall on the Tudor."

    She shook her head. "Why are you doing it? Thought you'd hired a crew."

    "They ran into a snag on their existing job, but I can't let that put my project behind schedule. Building inspector's coming tomorrow and it'd be at least a week before I could reschedule him."

    "How about if you head over and get started? I'll grab a pizza and six pack and deliver."

Logan tilted his head. "Don't you need to work?"

"Not as much as I need to eat." The design wasn't working anyway. It could wait until later tonight when she got home.

***

When Logan heard Savannah drive up, he put one final nail into the 2X4 and climbed off the ladder. He brushed sawdust off his jeans and swiped the back of his hand across his forehead as a tangy aroma filled the room. "Pepperoni."

She plopped the pizza box and a thermos onto the worn, red kitchen counter. "Figured coffee would be better than beer if we were working late. Sorry it took so long. Had to run by home and change."

He surveyed her denim overalls and soft pink tee shirt. Even matching pink high top sneakers. She flipped her ponytail over her shoulder and wrinkled her nose. "Do I have something on my face?"

"Uh, no." He blinked, trying to get a grip on the direction his mind headed. Her baggy outfit made a clear statement that she wasn't here for romance. Yet on Savannah, the denim overalls looked hotter than Victoria's Secret lingerie. He dusted his hands on his jeans. "I didn't...expect you to help."

She dug a couple plastic plates from a brown paper bag and placed a slice of pizza on each, then poured steaming coffee

Partners By Design

into two Styrofoam cups. "The least I could do. You have a deadline. We're partners, right?"

Partners? He hadn't counted on a partner when he'd leased her and Mallory the office, yet they were in a way. But his body craved another type of partnership tonight besides framing a damn wall.

Rich coffee aroma mingled with the pizza. His stomach growled and he grabbed a white cup off the counter, reminding himself to concentrate on satisfying his stomach and not his more carnal hunger.

Her cell phone chimed <u>You and Me Against The World.</u> Biting into his pizza, he waited until she finished listening to Constance Holt manipulate her with her cunning game before taking out his cell and dialing Savannah's number.

She stared at the phone and then at him. "Why are you calling me?"

"Trying to place the tune."

Her cheeks matched her pink shirt. "You don't recognize it?"

"It's familiar."

She downed a swig of coffee. "I'll change it. What's your favorite song?"

"What's that one?"

Opening the phone then shutting it and opening it again, she looked everywhere except at him. She jumped up and ran a hand over the wall. "Where do we start?"

Her discomfort only fed his curiosity. He sipped his coffee and watched her pace. Savannah Holt--not the nervous type. "The song title?"

"I Love a Rainy Night," she blurted out. "Okay? I'll change it."

The feel of Savannah in his arms that rainy night after the State Fair flashed into his mind--and lower. He wiped his sweaty hands on a napkin and stood. "Nah, I like that one. We better get busy."

He needed to focus on the work and forget Savannah was right next to him at every step. Her sweet perfume mixed with the smell of sawdust, creating erotic fantasies as she stretched to hold drywall in place while he nailed. She swept away scraps and sawdust as he worked. His coffee cup stayed hot and full.

How the hell could this sexy angel be Constance Holt's daughter?

Something scraped against the kitchen window.

She jumped and let go of the ladder. "What was that?"

He took in her wide-eyed expression. "Probably a limb. Wind's kicking up. Don't get all excited. No ghost."

"You never know," she said, wrapping her small hands around the ladder again.

"You sound disappointed." Why did he find her belief in ghosts so adorable?

Brushing against Savannah for the hundredth time, Logan leaned over and nailed the drywall, when what he really wanted to nail was a lot softer and sexier.

    As Savannah bent to pick up a nail he'd dropped, he tried not to stare at her ass. Was she driving him insane on purpose? She froze and stopped dead still, staring at the front door. "I definitely heard something."

    "What are you doing?" he asked, as she took off out the door.

    He jumped down off the ladder and followed. If she did hear something, she had no business confronting whoever it was on her own.

    "Look what I found," she said, bending down.

    "Let me guess, Casper?" he said, relieved that whatever the fuzzy thing was, it didn't seem to present a threat.

    She scooped the bundle into her arms and turned, holding the strangest looking dog he'd ever seen. "Isn't she adorable?"

    He tilted his head. "He." And adorable was far from how he'd describe the mutt she lugged inside and set on the floor. Skinny, wiry yellow hair and pointy ears.

    "We could call him Casper though." Savannah tore a small piece off the pizza and hand fed it to the dog. "How do you like that for a name, huh? You hungry, Casper?" she asked, feeding the mongrel a second bite.

    Casper's tail thumped against the

floor and he looked at Logan through sharp black eyes as if he didn't give a flip what she called him as long as the pizza kept coming.

Caving, Logan dug a Styrofoam cup out of the bag and filled it with water. "You thirsty, guy?" Holding the cup steady, he watched the long pink tongue drain every last drop and lick the floor where it splashed.

"Think we could keep him?" she asked, squatting down and rubbing Casper's head as she fed him another bite.

We? There was no 'we' in this equation.

As she stood, her wavy ponytail fell over her shoulder and disappeared, sandwiched between two round, t-shirt covered breasts and rough denim overalls.

God, just being in the same room with her had him so spun up, he couldn't think straight. No way could she not be feeling the same sexual pull. "Why are you doing this?" he demanded.

"Doing what?"

"Why are you here helping me?" he persisted.

"Because." She shrugged. "Because you helped me out last night. I wanted to reciprocate."

She couldn't be this naive. "What about your mother? What are you going to tell her?"

"This is none of her business."

"She'll make it her business. It may not be freakin' Prince Truesdale, but she's going to keep throwing rich guys at you until you latch onto one," Logan blurted out, picking up his nail gun then slamming it down on the ladder and glaring at her.

Her hands fisted on her hips. "There are other people besides myself to consider. What kind of person would I be if I didn't help my mom?"

This was bullshit. She was avoiding the issue. "Other people? There's you working your ass off to support her while she lunches on cucumber sandwiches and hobnobs with people who are entirely out of her league financially. What am I missing?"

"I promised my dad. I can't let her lose everything."

He'd called that one right. "So she's your personal charity case?"

"Me, Mom, and Chelsea have to look after each other."

"She wants to sell you to Truesdale to save her lifestyle because she's too lazy to get a job? I hardly think that's what your dad would want."

"You don't know her."

"She's a self-serving, manipulative bit--." He checked his anger. "user."

"Why do you hate her?"

Like he'd ever come clean about that one. "Look at what she's doing to you."

"She's my mother and I have to take care of her. The world does not revolve totally around me."

"No, it revolves totally around Constance."

Savannah turned and gathered up the remains of dinner, then shoved the pizza box and cups into the grocery bag. "I'm not listening to this."

He tried to wrangle the bag from her hand. "Savannah."

She yanked, but when he didn't release his hold, she let go. She took a deep breath, closed her eyes, then opened them and aquamarine orbs penetrated his soul. "Tell me what happened eight years ago, Logan."

He shut down. Stopped dead. The pepperoni churned in his stomach. He despised her mother, but not enough to destroy Savannah. "Past history. We're talking about now."

"No." She picked up her purse. "How can we discuss now until you come clean about the past?" Without waiting for an answer, she slammed out the door.

Logan stared at the door and then looked down and scratched Casper's head. "Word to the wise, Pal. Stay away from women."

* * *

When he heard his office door open, Logan clicked on 'Save' and looked up. Since her brakes were going out on the van, Savannah had taken his truck to check out a couple fabric stores and then buy a bed for the mutt.

As of two nights ago, he and Savannah were back to professional partners. Polite, but don't mention anything that wasn't business.

He wasn't sure where the hell their relationship, or non-relationship, stood but at least she hadn't pushed any more for an answer to the past.

"Hey, you're back. Find what you were looking for?" The temperature hadn't risen above freezing all day and was dropping fast. Perfect night for homemade stew from this little diner he'd discovered. He debated whether to pick up enough for Savannah too.

"Hello, Logan," Tom said from the doorway. "I take it Savannah isn't here yet."

So much for dinner. According to Savannah, she wasn't ready for a relationship, but Mr. Lexus sure as hell showed up on a regular basis. "Nope."

Tom took a seat on the sofa and stretched his legs in front of him as if hanging out in Logan's office was an everyday occurrence. "How about joining me at the club for dinner tonight?"

Logan narrowed his eyes. Why would this guy think Logan had any interest in joining him for an over-priced meal? They weren't buddies, not even friends. "Dinner?"

"Sure." Tom flashed a casual smile

and shuffled through the magazines on the table. "Got a proposition for you."

"Excuse me." They were attracted to the same woman and they both knew it, even if Savannah pretended to be oblivious. The best they could hope from dinner was to avoid a fistfight.

The guy made himself comfortable leafing through the latest copy of Architecture Journal. "Humor me."

Truesdale might as well have poked his finger in Logan's chest and shoved. Maybe that's what it took to wake him up.

If Logan didn't do something, Savannah was lost. But because of her blind spot for her damn manipulative mother, Savannah wasn't seeing the true picture. Again. In her mother and Truesdale's plastic world, Savannah's phenomenal spirit would succumb to a slow death.

Logan's blood turned to ice. For eight years he'd wondered, what if. Considering how they couldn't stop reacting to one another, he damn well knew they weren't done. And so did Savannah.

He'd been granted a second chance and if he didn't get off his ass, he was going to lie awake every night with nightmares about Prince Truesdale lying between Savannah's legs.

Logan grabbed his tie from the drawer and leather jacket off the chair back. He zipped his laptop into the case and met Tom's eyes. "After you."

Partners By Design

As Tom preceded him out of the building, they almost ran head on into Savannah coming in.

The object of the two men's affections shoved her windblown hair out of her face, and stared from Tom to Logan. "What's--?"

Before she finished her sentence, Tom smiled. "Nothing to worry you. Logan and I are going to dinner."

Savannah's eyes widened. "Why on earth would you two do that?"

Logan took his keys from her and headed for the truck. Let them work through it.

Savannah turned. "Logan, wait."

He ignored her, leaving Truesdale to deal with her. Savannah was so blind to how far her mother would go to keep them apart, that she would never figure out that Constance was driving this. But Logan knew. It was Constance's issue with Logan that had to be resolved. Tom Truesdale was just a pawn.

Strange though, Truesdale wasn't the one Logan had a beef with. Nor was Savannah or even her bitch of a mother.

If Logan lost Savannah a second time, it'd be his own damn fault.

Partners By Design

Chapter Fourteen

Had he lost his mind? Savannah glared at Tom as Logan's pickup started. "What are you up to?"

He reached for her arm. "Guy talk. A nice dinner at the club."

She jerked out of his grasp. "You and Logan? About me?"

He slid into his Lexus. "He and I can sort this out better without you there."

"There's nothing to sort out!" This was her life and he didn't think she needed to be included? She jumped in the passenger seat, punching in Logan's cell number. *Come on, pick up.* It rang five times and rolled to voice mail.

This little dinner would start out with awkward as an appetizer and move on to fiasco for a main course, with a side of boiling testosterone soup to spice things up.

Since her van was at home with iffy brakes, she'd ridden in with Mallory. "Look, I'm not sure what you plan to accomplish here, but just so we're clear, there *is* no you and me."

Tom's cell phone chimed and he held up one finger to silence her. He clipped

Partners By Design

the earpiece on and answered the phone as he pulled out of the lot.

Fifteen minutes and three phone calls later, Tom was still fixated on his cell and Logan still wasn't answering his.

* * *

Logan stood as Truesdale and Savannah entered. Savannah marched straight up to him. "Can I borrow you a second?" Her fingers closed around his wrist.

"Your table's ready, Mr. Truesdale," the hostess said.

Logan eased out of her grasp and followed Tom into the dining room.

This little meet and greet was an elaborate strategy in Truesdale's chess match, but for once Logan was in agreement. He was tired of playing the game. It was time for Savannah to see her mother for the user she was. Logan still had to deal with Constance, but first he needed to get Truesdale out of the picture once and for all.

He swallowed a dose of dread. Was forcing the issue his wisest move? His mind knew Savannah belonged with him, but could he live with the reality of Constance? Savannah's desperate, bankrupt mother was going to add a whole new level to mother-in-law from hell.

Logan hung his leather jacket over the back of the chair and straightened his tie. This morning when he'd put on khaki Dockers and a black sport shirt for breakfast with a client, he hadn't planned

Partners By Design

on a country club confrontation for dinner.

Savannah didn't open her mouth, just glared at each of them in turn. Truesdale led with pretty much a balance sheet of how well his business was doing. Who the hell cared how many zillion time-share units he'd sold? Why didn't he just cut to the chase? Constance was pulling the puppet strings or he wouldn't have orchestrated this party. Logan waited, debating the wisdom of tossing the first match to the powder keg.

"Excuse me." Savannah scooted out of the chair and headed toward the lady's room. Both arms were crossed over her stomach and Logan wasn't sure whether she was sick or just needed time to calm down.

Tom frowned and faced Logan. "I can't get this woman to give me the time of day. Your reappearance in her life obviously has something to do with her reluctance."

Logan folded his arms across his chest. He sure as hell hoped so.

Tom's voice rose. "Look, you seem like a nice guy and I get how easy it is to fall in love with Savannah. But are you prepared to support her and Constance?"

"So this is about Savannah's mother?"

Tom shook his head. "I'm going to level with you."

<u>Level with me?</u> Flashing red bullshit indicator.

"You can't afford them. I'm already paying Constance's bills." Tom shrugged.

187

"But I'm not complaining. That's just the way things work in this circle."

Logan raised an eyebrow.

Savannah's mother was bartering her away like a prize statue at an auction. But what bothered him more was that Savannah was letting her get away with it. The girl he'd fallen in love with would have shut anyone down who tried to manipulate her, even her own mother. "Is Savannah aware of that?"

"Of course. They need a man to keep things afloat." Tom leveled his dark brown eyes on Logan. "What do you have to offer them? You don't comprehend what you're buying into here. Cut your losses. Walk away."

Logan's fingers dug into his thighs. "Not going to happen."

As Savannah approached, he studied her soft, flawlessly made up face. What had happened to that fiery sixteen-year-old girl?

Tom leaned halfway across the table and the right corner of his lip snarled like an attack dog. "Back away from her."

Logan set his jaw, stood, and took Savannah's hand. "Dance?"

* * *

Savannah followed Logan onto the dance floor, anxious for the first chance she'd had to talk to him alone. She straightened his black tie against his black shirt, placed her hand on his shoulder, and stared into his stoic

Partners By Design

expression. "What the hell is going on here?"

"War games."

She tilted her head. "What does that mean?"

"Choose. I don't give a shit how much money he gave your mother, make it clear. Tell him to get the hell out of your life. Give me a chance." He pressed his lips to hers, drawing her bottom lip into his mouth. She whimpered as he ran his tongue across the lip and released it.

Tom tapped Logan's shoulder. "I'm cutting in."

Logan's navy blue eyes never left her, but he didn't speak.

"You two are drawing attention," Tom said, easing Savannah away from Logan.

Logan narrowed one eye at him. "Get your hands off her."

"This is asinine. You are both acting like cavemen." Savannah pulled away, nervous Logan might throw a punch if Tom said one more word.

Tom glared at Logan. "So, you *are* sleeping with her?"

"Stop!" She wanted to bang their heads together. "Why can't two educated men, even in the most civilized environment, have a discussion without testosterone kicking in? Why don't you just each take fifty paces, turn and shoot?"

Logan jabbed a hand through his hair

Partners By Design

and growled. "Tom's no different than your mother. She tried to make you into a socialite. He plans to turn socialite Savannah into a trophy wife. And you just roll with the flow so he'll pay mom's bills."

Savannah seethed. "My or my mother's finances are none of your concern, Logan. But just so I'm clear, what do *you* want to make me into?"

Tom stepped between them, facing Logan. "You need to lower your voice. She's right. What I do for Savannah or her mother is none of your concern."

"Then why did you make a point to tell me, Slick?"

Maybe there wasn't anything she could do to save them from making fools of themselves, but she didn't have to stand here and be party to their insanity. Had it penetrated either of their rock hard skulls that she'd make her own decision?

She eased back a step, watching the two men positioning nose to nose. So focused on their battle, they didn't even notice when she backed away a couple more steps.

Using the crowded dance floor as cover, she wove her way outside and smiled at the parking valet. "Tom Truesdale's silver Lexus please. I'm sorry, I don't have the ticket."

The walkie-talkie squawked as he pushed the button. "It'll be right up, Ms. Holt."

"Thank you." She fished her last ten-dollar bill out of her slacks pocket and shoved it into his hand before he graciously seated her behind the wheel.

* * *

Logan caught a flash of royal blue and turned in time to see Savannah race out the door. "Shit." He reached into his slacks pocket and realized his keys were in his jacket. Ignoring Tom, he bolted for the table and grabbed his leather jacket off the back of the chair.

"What's going on?" Truesdale asked, sounding as if he'd just returned from the john and realized he'd missed a critical scene in the movie.

They hadn't even ordered, but Logan tossed a couple bills on the table and gathered Savannah's purse and coat. He reached the front of the club just in time to watch the Lexus taillights disappear into the fog.

Tom skidded to a stop beside him, shoving his arms into his overcoat. "Was that my car?"

Logan rubbed his forehead and hid a grin. "Yeah. Should have seen that one coming." He shrugged at Truesdale. "Need a lift?"

The guy stared into the eerie night, and then raised both hands. "Sure, why not."

Logan held his tongue as Truesdale, still wearing a bemused frown, followed him to the truck.

Partners By Design

Tom brushed imaginary crumbs off the vinyl and fished the seat belt out from the crack in the seat before climbing in. "You knew what she was going to do?"

Starting the engine, Logan gave Truesdale time to get buckled in. "The night we met, Savannah caught her boyfriend banging her best friend. She stole both their clothes and took off in her new Miata, which she didn't know how to drive. And if that hadn't hooked me, after I rescued her in her stalled car she pulled a wallet out of the jerkwad's jeans and bought me dinner."

"Savannah wouldn't steal a man's pants."

This evening was turning out to be more enjoyable than it had started. "Pay attention. She just stole your Lexus, Pal."

Tom clasped his hands together. "So you had sex with her that night?"

Looking back, Logan considered how close they'd come. "It was her sixteenth birthday," he said, leaving Tom to wonder. "I taught her to drive a stick shift."

Tom massaged his temples. "You were both just kids. It was puppy love."

It wasn't, but Logan saw no gain in debating the point. He shifted gears and turned down Camp Bowie Boulevard toward Savannah's house. "I don't care what Constance Holt has in mind. I'm not walking away."

"Neither am I," Tom said. "Savannah

fascinates me." Truesdale stared out the window into the fog. "I can't figure out why she won't accept my help."

Wow, even guys with mega-millions had issues. So Savannah hadn't accepted his money, but Constance had.

Truesdale closed his eyes. "Let's just find my car."

There were only two places to look for Savannah and since her van wasn't at the office Logan figured her house was the best shot. When he parked at the curb, the Lexus was in the drive, the lights glowing in the eerie fog like some possessed demon.

Truesdale let out a breath. "So where do we go from here? I don't lose at business and I'll be damned if I'm going to lose Savannah."

"Yeah? Well everybody has to lose sometime." Logan stepped out and leaned against the truck, monitoring Savannah's temperament as she exited the Lexus and headed across the yard.

She tossed Truesdale the keys. "If you two are any smarter than you look, you'll leave without opening your mouths."

Logan held his tongue as Truesdale caught the keys then reached for her hand. "We need to talk."

"Go." Savannah didn't flinch.

The guy backed away. Still watching her, he got into the Lexus and started the engine.

"You too." She shot Logan a frigid glare and stomped toward the house.

He retrieved her purse and coat from the pickup and pulled out her house key. Following her onto the porch, he kept one eye on the driveway. The Lexus hadn't budged, and no doubt wouldn't until the pickup did.

Savannah's shoulders and back were rigid as she faced the door and waited Logan out. She turned and held out her hand.

Reaching around her, he unlocked the door and pushed it open, then stepped back.

She entered, but still looked ready to explode.

He draped the coat over her arm and placed the purse in her hand.

Savannah felt numb as she dropped her belongings on the end table, but she remained in the doorway and faced Logan. She wasn't sure what to say to him, how to make him understand. The problem was that he did understand. "Not tonight."

Instead of the anticipated temper, Logan cupped one hand against her cheek in a seductive caress. "Give it up. You can't force yourself to fall in love with someone."

"Not anymore than you can decide when to fall in love." In that way, they had both under-estimated the power of this thing between them.

Partners By Design

He leaned in and took his time seducing her mouth into submission. His other hand circled her waist and urged her close, molding his body to hers.

She closed her eyes and let it happen, reveled in the pressure of his hand at the small of her back.

Her fingers slid around his neck, tangling in his hair, spanning the width of his neck, and tugging him closer. Tilting her head, she ran her tongue over his teeth.

Heat pooled between her legs. She gave the magnetic pull free reign and pressed against him, closing her eyes and absorbing the full impact of his seduction. Their bodies melded. Yin and yang.

Logan pulled away, touched his tongue to his top lip, and returned her stare. "I'm done playing. We've got to deal with this soon." He spun on his heels and headed for his truck.

She'd never heard that edge from Logan, but she had no doubt she was operating on borrowed time.

She watched him walk away, then closed the door, and leaned against it. She'd never had two men face off over her before. It wasn't as flattering as in the movies. And damn Logan, he didn't fight fair. He knew he could melt her with just a touch.

Mallory raced out of Savannah's bedroom, a long terry robe flapping behind her like a purple cape, Casper on her heels. "I was watching out the window. You driving Tom's Lexus and Tom riding with Logan! What's up with that?"

"A testosterone epidemic." Savannah's emotions bubbled just below the boiling point. "I could throttle them both."

Casper dropped to his butt and tilted his head at Savannah.

"Tell Tom to get lost." Mallory sauntered fully into the room, looping the belt on her robe.

Savannah's head jerked up to stare at her friend. That might be a little easier if her mother didn't owe the man $10,000 dollars. Savannah massaged the back of her neck.

"It's obvious to everyone, including both men, that you and Logan are far from finished."

Swallowing a lump lodged in her throat, Savannah closed her eyes. "It's not that simple."

"I don't get it. Do you crave a lifetime membership to the country club so you can rub elbows with elitist? Bridge on Tuesday. Tennis on Thursday. A professional trainer to keep your figure fit for the latest fads. Nothing wrong with that, if it's what...."

"I love Logan!"

Mallory closed her mouth and tilted her head. "Okay?"

Savannah couldn't stop her chin from quivering. "Tom is around because my mother is making sure he sticks around. But if I never saw Tom again I'd be fine. Logan..."

Tears ran down Savannah's face. She'd never verbalized the depth of her hurt or even allowed it into her conscious thought. It would be easier to marry Tom for his money than to admit the truth. He was a buffer against Logan. "Nobody has ever had the kind of power over me that Logan Reid does."

"I'm pretty sure that goes along with love."

Savannah struggled to speak above a whisper. "What if I give Logan another chance and he leaves me again? There wouldn't even be enough pieces to pick up."

"Sometimes you just have to take a chance. What makes you so sure Logan would leave you?"

"He did before and eight years later he still won't tell me why!" Savannah swiped away the tears but she couldn't meet her friend's eyes. Casper nudged at Savannah's hand and she scratched his head. Now she'd even managed to upset the dog.

"Well, that was a long time ago. Either you trust him," Mallory stared at her and blew out a breath, "or you let him go."

Partners By Design

Chapter Fifteen

    Giving Savannah time to cool down after the club scene last night might not have been Logan's wisest move. Yet, she had to make her own decision and forcing her hand wouldn't work in his favor any more than it would Truesdale's.

    He pulled into the office parking lot for the first time since seven this morning. Under the illusion that physical labor would alleviate his frustration, he'd spent the day at a jobsite, running power tools and pounding nails. It hadn't worked any better than his plan to stay away from Savannah.

    Forget it. Grabbing his laptop, he locked the truck and squared his shoulders. He wasn't hiding out here and avoiding *his* office because of Savannah's inability to stand up to her mother and dump Truesdale. It was already time he should be headed home for a good night's sleep and he still had a day's work to accomplish. "Come on, boy."

    Casper followed him inside and plopped down on the rug in front of his desk. This dog was too well trained to not belong to someone. He'd been by Logan's side since he'd taken him from Mallory early this morning. No leash and yet he'd never ventured more than a few feet away. Maybe Logan could keep his eyes focused long enough to get a couple hours work done before he collapsed.

* * *

Savannah smoothed her skirt and watched as Tom entered the exclusive little restaurant. *She'd* invited *him* to dinner, so why were her nerves shot? Just remember, tonight she was in the driver's seat.

Talking into his ever-present phone, his gaze scanned the dozen or so tables. Still carrying on his conversation, he smiled when he spotted her. To his credit, he ended the call and clicked the phone off before taking his seat. "Good evening."

"Hi." Courage. Just say the words.

"It's off." Tom flashed his smile and slid the phone into his breast pocket. "I'm all yours. I promise."

She grinned. "Thanks, but the phone's not a problem."

He held up one finger before she could elaborate. "First, let me say how flattering it is to receive a dinner invitation from such a gorgeous lady."

Oh God, don't go there. Quickly before he got the wrong idea. "We need to talk."

"Sounds ominous," he said, placing his napkin in his lap.

"We have to figure out a payment plan

Partners By Design

so I can repay the money you loaned Mom."

"No, we don't. That agreement was between Constance and myself. Nothing to do with you." He smiled and reached across the table and took her hand, began massaging her ring finger. "Look, I realize things have been hectic and I haven't been as attentive as I should, especially at the crucial beginning of a relationship. I even take the blame for you drifting toward Logan."

"Tom, wait!" This train was barreling full speed down the wrong track.

Still smiling, he pulled velvet, ring-size box from his coat pocket.

Panic shot through her.

He opened the lid and an enormous mass of diamonds twinkled from a platinum setting. "Do you like it?"

She jerked her hand away and clenched her fist. "No!" No. This wasn't going the way she'd planned. Savannah wrung her hands. "What are you doing?" she stammered. So much for handling this with class. "I'm sorry. You misconstrued my invitation. I wanted to sit down over a nice dinner and talk, explain, but..." She gathered her courage. "I've tried to be upfront. We're not...I'm not..." His image blurred through her tears. She'd screwed this all up.

"Shhh. Calm down. You were up front." He reached across the table and recaptured her hand. "You were clear from the beginning that you needed the contacts."

She shook her head, forced herself to look him in the eye. "Tom, I deliberately used you as a buffer between me and Logan. And that wasn't fair."

"Logan." His jaw stiffened.

This hurt more than she'd expected. "You're a wonderful guy."

"Ahh, those pretty, nice words that every man dreads." He stared down at the table and rubbed his eyes.

She gulped, trying to use clearer words to make her point. She felt like the world's greenest scum for using him.

"Savannah." He placed a finger under her chin and tilted it. "Let me take care of you. You need someone now and Logan can't do that, at least not for years to come."

As the words registered, her heart ached for him. "Did you ever think that the reason women only want you for your money is because you believe that's all you have to offer?"

He closed his eyes, and his self-assured expression faded. "When you're in my position, that's what people see."

"Don't settle for that. Wait until you find a woman who doesn't see the money, or at least doesn't care."

"Funny. That's what fascinated me about you." He stared at her a long minute then cocked a brow. "He must be a hell of a guy."

"He burns in my soul." She blinked

back tears, not wanting to hurt Tom, but realizing there was no avoiding it. "You'll find someone like that."

Tom sighed. "I thought I had."

* * *

Casper's head shot up from where he was sleeping beside the desk just as Logan heard a key turn in the front office. Why would either of his suite mates return after nine on Friday night?

"Savannah." He blinked at the royal blue cape, not sure whether she was reality or fantasy. Her hair was clipped up on top of her head in a loose sort of ponytail.

She locked the door in the dim reception area and leaned against it. He couldn't decipher her mood with the limited light coming from his office and she didn't bother to turn on more.

She pushed away from the door and sauntered toward him. Rubbing Casper's head, she pulled a treat out of her purse and handed it to him. "Hey boy, you enjoy your treat while I talk to Logan, okay?" She gave his head one more pat then shut the door, leaving the dog in the reception area.

Just inside his office door, she dropped her purse and blue cape. She stood in front of him wearing a pair of tight jean shorts and a bright pink crop top that didn't quite reach the waistband of the shorts. She kicked her matching pink sandals off before she ran her hands up Logan's arms and around his neck.

God, don't let her be playing me. I'm not strong enough to walk away, not again.

His eyes feasted on the skimpy outfit and the way it clung to her curves, an outfit reminiscent of the night they'd met. Holding her was torture and heaven. Something had changed, but he wasn't sure whether it was good or bad.

But she was in his arms, not Truesdale's.

A tendril of perfume-scented hair tickled his chin and her breath cooled his neck. He leaned around and kissed her temple. "You going to tell me why you're here?"

"No." She tilted her head back and her eyes glistened with tears. "You're a smart man."

His mind struggled to understand what was happening, what she'd just said. "Be explicit."

Her body slithered against his chest as she threaded her fingers in his hair. "Shhh, Logan. No more talking." Her glossy lips opened over his and erased any doubt he might have had about the wisdom of allowing her to get close.

He didn't try to tell himself everything would work out. He had no idea if it would. The only thing that mattered tonight was that she was here with him.

Her tongue in his mouth and the distinctive taste of Savannah. The pressure of her breasts against his chest. Her small hands caressing his neck.

Intoxicating whiffs of expensive perfume. Kisses so deep he couldn't breathe.

Standing on tiptoe, she stood almost his height. The low, tight neckline of her shirt left the top of her breasts exposed. He gave into the temptation and brushed his knuckles across her cleavage, feeling her every breath. He ran his hands over her body, palming her breasts through the soft cotton and feeling her heat against his aroused body.

"Spark any memories?" she asked taking his hand and placing it on her denim covered ass. She ran one hand beneath his shirt and hooked the other inside the waistband of his jeans.

No longer trying to control his desire, he unzipped her shorts and worked them lower until he grasped her silky hips. Her skin sizzled. When she arched her back and nuzzled that feline body into his he almost purred. "Memories of that May we met."

Threading his fingers beneath the scrap of white lace panties, he ground his body against hers. He slid her panties down her thighs and those mile long legs.

He hoisted her onto the edge of his desk, leaned forward, and grabbed the box of condoms from his desk drawer.

A bit of a challenge as she took that opportunity to unzip his jeans and push them down over his hips. For a second, he lost track of what he was doing.

"You could work with me here." He ripped the cellophane packet with his

Partners By Design

teeth.

"Just get the thing on," she said, kissing her way around his ear and snuggling into his neck. The tip of her tongue sent exquisite shivers along his collarbone.

His mouth watered and he struggled for air as she moved against him. His dreams had been filled with Savannah all of his adult life. All he could think about was being inside her again.

She arched and locked her legs tight around his waist. "I need you."

He pulled her shirt off one shoulder, and kneaded her breast, but he couldn't stop moving. *Let her enjoy this as much as I am.* His jeans bunched around his thighs and prevented full movement, but Savannah hadn't given him time to prepare.

"Don't slow down," she panted, rubbing against him like a tigress, purring and moaning, moving her hips with his. Skin slapped against skin, but she was relentless as she clutched his hips and strived for deeper, faster, harder. Blood pulsed through his veins when she cried out and he followed her into ecstasy. It took an acrobat's coordination to stay on his feet.

Before he recovered from their first skirmish, she yanked his tee shirt over his head in preparation for round two. He returned the favor, leaving a real live goddess standing in front of him. His eyes clouded over as they looked up her slender frame.

His lungs shut down at the dark triangle at the juncture of her thighs. Her nipples tightened as his gaze roamed upward and he wondered if he would survive her.

Savannah reveled in the feel of Logan. They lay on his navy leather couch wrapped in a peach throw she kept in her office. Skin to skin, nothing between them to lessen the closeness. His hands were calloused and rough. He rubbed his cheek against her neck and nuzzled lower. The late night stubble reminded her he was real. This was real. She tilted her head into his hand and ran her hand over his pecs as he nibbled her neck. His mouth traveled to her breast, the warmth making her nipple bead.

She snuggled against him. No words were adequate to describe being with Logan Reid. Heaven was too calm. Exquisite was too controlled. Hot came close, but what about the tenderness? The rightness?

She needed this. She needed Logan. He completed her. She ran a bare foot up the inside of his leg and closed her eyes.

His skin was tight and tasted salty. His scent clean and masculine.

Strands of sweat-dampened hair stuck to her face and she didn't have an ounce of energy left to even push it aside, but she wasn't finished with him.

With one hand on each side of her face, Logan combed her hair back and kissed her hard as she maneuvered on top.

He cupped her bottom and held her tight against him.

This was where she belonged. This man knew the real Savannah. Possibly better than she knew herself. He knew she struggled to pay the bills. He knew about her mother's circumstances. And best of all he preferred her true situation to the one her mother had fabricated in order for her to land a rich husband.

* * *

As the first rays of morning sun turned night to day, Logan unwound a lock of Savannah's long brown hair from around his neck. He'd been awake awhile, just enjoying holding her. It was a little tough to breathe with her draped across his chest, but he wasn't complaining. One hand was around his neck and the other trapped under his back, between the couch cushions. Her hair was tangled across his chest. The blanket just covered her ass and his eyes feasted on her slender shoulders and back.

He jerked as Casper barked and he heard the distinctive creak of the front door to the suite.

"Good morning, Casper. What are you doing sleeping out here?" Mallory chirped from the reception area. "I saw Logan and Savannah's vehicles in the parking lot. They're both getting an early start."

His office door was shut, but not locked. "Savannah, wake up. We've got company," he whispered, giving her a shake.

She bolted off him. "Who?"

He left a layer of flesh as he peeled his bare back off the leather cushion.

"Anybody here?" Mallory asked.

Savannah tossed him his jeans and struggled into her panties and tank top.

He scooped her shorts off the floor and handed them to her then tugged on his jeans. "What time is it?"

"I have no idea, but it's got to be after nine for Mallory to be here on a Saturday."

"Where's my shirt?" He looked from the couch to the table.

She fished it out from under his desk. Giving him a long kiss, she laid a hand against his cheek. She pressed the shirt into his hand and padded barefoot out the door. "Hurry."

"Wait." Stuffing his arms into the shirt, he followed close on her heels.

Mallory turned from her office and looked from Savannah to Logan. Her amazement widened into an amused grin at Savannah's skimpy summer ensemble. She held up a plastic container. "I brought homemade cinnamon rolls. Don't guess anybody's made coffee."

"I'm on it," Logan said, stumbling toward the kitchen. He needed a few minutes to pull himself together and he'd just as soon Savannah handled Mallory's inquisition.

Savannah shook her head as Logan made

his escape. Typical man. She stopped short. Ok, so there was nothing typical about Logan. He shattered all her preconceptions about men. He understood her need to make her business succeed on her own. He'd known Tom was wrong for her even before she was willing to admit it.

"I'll give you a cinnamon roll if you tell me everything." Mallory opened the container and placed it on the desk. The calorie heavy, wonderful sticky aroma of hot cinnamon bread made Savannah want to pounce. She'd missed dinner last night.

"Are you going to leave me in suspense?" Mallory tapped her foot.

Savannah's face heated just thinking about last night. But before she could answer, the dog growled low in his throat.

Constance burst through the door, hands waving and that motherly, concerned frown on her face. "You *are* here. I stopped by the house but there was nobody home."

Still groggy, Savannah glanced at the wall clock. What was her mother even doing out of bed at nine-thirty, much less dressed and paying an impromptu visit?

She scaled Savannah's appearance and reached out and tugged on a lock of her hair. She turned silently and watched Logan come out of the kitchen.

Savannah cringed as Constance's gaze scaled Logan from his tousled hair to his bare feet. His shirt was buttoned but not tucked in and he still had that just crawled out of bed, sleepy eyed look.

Savannah curled her toes in a futile effort to hide her own bare feet. Her hair hadn't been combed since yesterday afternoon. No doubt Logan's lovemaking had erased every trace of makeup. At least she'd dressed, but that didn't shield her from feeling nude and exposed under her mom's harsh scrutiny.

"You didn't." Her mother's fists clenched so tight her knuckles were bone white. Constance's distorted fury morphed into a smile more barracuda than human. "Obviously you need a shower and some clean clothes. I'll follow you home." She scowled at Casper who had planted himself between mother and daughter. "Where did that mongrel come from?"

"We found him," Logan answered.

Constance's gaze shifted from dog to man without changing disgusted expression.

Savannah padded into Logan's office, with Casper dogging her heels as if he could protect her. She retrieved her purse, and looked around for anything she might have left. The last thing she wanted was a confrontation between her mother and Logan. Mom had always hated him for breaking Savannah's heart. And now in her warped mind, she'd blame Logan for Savannah's lack of interest in Tom.

Logan entered his office behind her. "Don't go with her."

She slung the cape around her shoulders and slipped her bare feet into her sandals. "Better to face her now than to put it off."

"I'll tag along."

Touched at his desire to protect her, she leaned forward and kissed him on the lips. "I appreciate the offer, but it'd only make things worse. Give her time. I'll call you."

"Ahem." Constance cleared her throat from the doorway and the dog positioned himself between her and Savannah, never taking his eyes off the older woman. "You ready?" Constance asked.

Savannah stared from Constance's folded arms to Logan's frigid glare. Mom had always resented Logan, but something about his expression nagged at her. She didn't have time to dwell on that though until she diffused her mother.

Giving Logan's hand a quick squeeze, she followed Mom out of the office. Today was not the day to play peacemaker.

Chapter Sixteen

Savannah pulled into her drive and Constance's Caddie whipped in behind her. At least the van was running. This week. She sucked in a breath and tried to keep a grip on her temper. They might be in this financial war together, but their approaches differed. Same side or not, this was going to be a battle.

The Cadillac door slammed and Mom stomped across the lawn and onto the porch. Savannah pulled her keys from the ignition and followed, her mind scrambling for a way to discharge Mom's intense anger.

The ancient lock on the old house rattled and her hand shook, but she managed to open the front door.

Constance preceded her inside. "What have you done? What were you thinking?"

"Mom, just sit down and let's discuss this."

"You've trashed everything we've worked so hard for and you want to talk?" Constance grabbed her arm and her voice escalated. "Did you end it with Tom yesterday afternoon?"

Trying unsuccessfully to yank free, Savannah gave up. "Yes, but..."

"Savannah, this obsession of yours about making it on your own is admirable to a point, but it's bordering on absurd. The most sought after bachelor in Fort Worth is pursuing you and you turned him away for a nobody."

Savannah steamed. "So you're saying I should date a man I don't love just because he's rich and let the man I do love get away a second time?"

Constance shook her head. "Logan Reid? How could you ever trust him after what he did to you? Just because he stole your virginity, you've deluded yourself into believing you're still in love with him."

"I don't *think* I love Logan. I know I love him."

Constance's manicured fingernails dug into Savannah's arm. "Love fades fast when you're broke. Your sister understood after the money dried up when Daddy died. You are young and attractive. Find the right man. This is our survival!" Constance shrieked, becoming more frantic with each syllable.

"For once, this isn't about you." That didn't come out right.

Constance's eyes filled with tears. "Is that the lie Logan is filling your head with? You think I want you to go with Tom just to benefit me?"

"Don't you?" Savannah blinked. For the first time she noticed wrinkles creasing the corners of her mother's eyes and lips. The woman was terrified her looks would fade before she landed a husband to take care of her. "Mom, I love you, but it isn't up to you to choose who I'm with."

"You threw away everything I've spent your father's life insurance on for one night with a well-hung loser."

"That's not fair. Logan is so much more than a one-night stand. He gets me. I'm the real Savannah with him." Savannah didn't know how to make her mother understand, but she wasn't going to give up Logan. "I'm sorry Dad's money is gone, but at some point you have to work for things like everyone else." It could be years before she had the funds to help Mom. "I'll try to kick in a few bucks, but I can't even support myself yet, much less your lifestyle."

Mom's green eyes became wild. "I can't watch you do this. If this is the real Savannah, you aren't even my daughter." She turned, stiffened her back, and flounced out the front door.

Savannah raced across the room as Constance bolted down the stoop. "Oh yes I am. But unlike you, I won't live my life in fear of ending up back in a rusted out trailer!"

Mom turned, her glare cold and unrelenting. "You are going to live to regret your actions. When I suggested you screw Logan's brains out and get over him, I didn't mean to dump Tom."

Bitch! Savannah flinched as the Caddie door slammed and the powerful V8

Partners By Design

revved, and then roared down the street, missing the fender of Logan's truck by a hair.

Logan's truck!

Logan waited, leaning against his pickup at the curb. Casper sat inside the cab. Logan's gaze followed the departing Caddie, then turned back to Savannah.

She shook her head and wrapped both arms around her stomach, ashamed to face him. Ashamed of her mother's hateful words. Ashamed of what he must be thinking. As he approached and she looked up into Logan's eyes, Savannah's heart broke.

"Screw my brains out and get over me?" One corner of his mouth tilted up in his crooked grin that never failed to melt her insides. "How'd that work out for you?"

"Oh, Logan. You know that wasn't what last night was about..."

"I know." He put one finger to her lips then covered them with his. The love inside her exploded. She slipped her arms inside the warmth of his black hooded sweatshirt and rubbed her face against the soft cotton.

Why couldn't her mother be happy for her? "I never meant to hurt anybody. Not you. Not her."

"Your mom is a piece of work." He threaded his fingers through the hair at the nape of her neck and massaged. "Nobody has the right to expect you to change your life to please them when they won't even risk chipping a nail. You're setting yourself up for failure trying to live up to her expectations."

"I know you don't believe this, but she loves me. Beneath all the hoopla she puts on for the world, is my mom. My choices may cause her to lose her home. Her home!" She pulled away and wiped her face. She needed him to understand. "Just before Daddy died, he told me he bought her that house for security, to guarantee that she'd always have a real home."

"I don't think he meant to lay that kind of responsibility on you or for you to give up your dreams for hers. This isn't about your mother loving you. It's about you selling out to pay her bills."

For whatever reason, and there had to be some psychological babble with a name as long as the Caddie, she had to defend the woman who'd given birth to her. "All she's ever had to bank on is her looks and they're fading. She's alone and broke."

"So, since she isn't having any luck snaring a sugar daddy, you have to become her meal ticket? And then will your daughter do the same for you?"

Savannah blinked at the truth in his summation. Mom did want a meal ticket. Tom wanted to play the hero. Everyone wanted something. Savannah's emotions bubbled to the surface as she pushed away and blinked at Logan. "How are you different? What do you want from me?"

Logan stuffed his hands in his

pockets and his face became guarded. "I don't want anything from you," he snapped.

His words knocked the air out of her. "Fine!" She turned and stormed toward the door, determined to get away from him before she humiliated herself and turned into a blubbering idiot. She grabbed the knob and yanked the storm door, but before it opened, Logan's hand slammed it shut.

His arms caged her in and his chest pressed warm against her back. She flattened her palms against the cool glass to try and maintain enough space to breathe.

"I want a lover, a friend, and a partner," he whispered into her hair.

Her body shuddered and she closed her eyes to block out the tears, but they squeezed between her lashes and trickled down her cheeks. "Me too."

Logan held her until she quit shaking. Slowly she turned and wrapped her arms around his waist. The cold morning air nipped at her bare skin. "How about a hot shower?"

"Mmm. Works for me." He turned her toward the door and followed her inside.

* * *

Savannah inhaled the tangy scent of sage and leaned against the warmth of Logan's side as they strolled along the rock paths in the Botanic Gardens. "Thanks for suggesting lunch. I guess I was hungry after all." The Garden's Restaurant always had exquisite lunch entrees, but the best part had been the serenity Logan offered by simply being quiet and letting her initiate the conversation, or not.

His arm tightened around her shoulders as they strolled down the stone path, communicating his support better than any amount of words.

The dog plodded along beside them, sniffing at his surroundings, even though it meant wearing his new red collar. A squirrel scampered across the path and he sprinted ahead, jerking his leash.

"Whoa, boy." Logan tightened his grip, stopping the dog in mid-jump. Casper's ears pricked and he sat, but stared at the squirrel as it raced up a tree and turned to chatter.

Savannah slipped her hand beneath Logan's sweatshirt and spread her fingers against his bare back. The sky was clear blue, but the temperature had dropped into the upper forties. Yet there was something grounding about the blustery breeze and being with Logan that reminded her she was alive.

Water trickled over the meandering waterfall and she breathed deep and tried to let the sound seep in to calm her jitters. "Maybe I over-reacted. She did help pay for my education."

"Her choice."

"You never liked her," she said, more stating fact than accusing.

"True. She plays mind games on you with this whole 'I did all this for you'

Partners By Design

BS."

She knew he was right, but she hadn't finished talking through it. "She only wanted what was best for me."

He turned the collar up on her jacket and snuggled her against his chest. "She helped put you through college so you'd feel obligated to support her. Might have been good for you, but it was more for her financial benefit."

She tilted her head and looked at his strong, independent profile as the wind ruffled his hair, reminding her of when he was younger. "Don't you resent your parents not helping pay for your education?"

"I didn't want anything from them. Not then. Not now. Say what you will about my drunken old man, he taught me independence."

Casper lost interest in the squirrel and tugged on the leash. Logan let him lead them to a pond where he could bark at the giant goldfish wiggling through the water. She watched the dog, his butt up in the air and tail whipping back and forth in anticipation. She could relate as she leaned against Logan's chest, well maybe not to the tail wagging, but certainly to the anticipation. For the first time since they'd met again, she felt as if she and Logan had a chance for a future together. "We could go back to my place. Mallory is headed to Quentin's and won't be back until Monday."

"Now there's a plan I can get into,"

he said, pulling Casper away from the pond.

* * *

"Dammit!" The suite door slammed.

Logan stood as Savannah charged into his office Monday evening like a sexy human whirlwind.

"I just got fired!" She flung her purse on the sofa, snatched the Nerf ball off the table, and paced as she ranted. "He said that if my own business was so important and was taking so much time away from my job, that maybe I no longer needed Windows To Go."

Casper dove under the desk and rested his head on the floor between his front paws trying to melt into the wood floor. Those pointy ears sticking straight up might make that a little difficult.

Squeezing the ball as if strangling her boss' neck, Savannah growled. "Who does he think he is?" She didn't seem to be looking for a response, only an audience, as she paused long enough to suck in a breath.

His body heated to her fire, even if she was pissed off.

"I've busted my buns for that jerk and this is my reward. Two weeks pay and an escort out the door."

Flopping onto the sofa, she took a deep breath and released the defenseless ball. "I'm so freakin' sunk! Like a measly two weeks is going to make a dent in my bills."

She jabbed her fingers through her hair and scrunched up her cute little nose. Having never been fired, he wasn't sure how someone was supposed to react, but he was pretty sure he'd be quietly licking his wounds and sulking, not broadcasting it loud enough for the entire building to hear.

She looked so damn hot.

The universe aligned.

He stared at her flushed face and windblown hair, then swallowed hard as his mind cleared. Savannah was back in his life and this time she was here to stay. He wasn't losing her without a fight. And there would be a fight.

"I hated that job!" She yanked a throw pillow off the sofa and twisted it like a washrag. "But I can't survive without the paycheck."

This isn't high school. It isn't even hot, burn in hell lust. I'm in long haul, forever after, growing old together, and rocking chairs love with Savannah.

For the first time she slowed long enough to acknowledge he was in the office. "What am I going to do now, Logan?"

What am I going to do, Savannah? He walked across and dropped down beside her on the sofa. "We'll drum up business, cut expenses, and make it work. Together." He was talking about more than the business. This was a real relationship.

"You knock the breath out of me." He

had to kiss her. Now. Cupping her exquisite, ticked off face between his hands, he leaned forward and opened his mouth over hers.

She turned to him and straddled his lap. "I can relate to that."

Ignoring the immediate problem, he tilted his head and kissed her again, desperate for the feel of her, the taste. "Come home with me."

* * *

Logan yanked his shirt over his head without unbuttoning it, eager to have Savannah in his bed. As he cradled the back of her head and eased her onto the pillow, his only thoughts were the million things he'd fantasized about doing to her, with her. She arched her back and pulled him down on top. He'd never wanted a woman like he craved her. Her body was warm and willing beneath him as he wedged one hand behind her and unclasped her lacy pink bra. Her tongue ran up his neck and around the back of his ear, before tantalizing his lips.

His mind was as filled with Savannah as his arms were. Her beauty. Her vulnerability. Her all-consuming allure. "Touch me."

Her hand was already struggling with the snap on his jeans. As she pushed his boxers down over his hips, he moved into her hand and tried to convince himself they had a chance in hell of making this relationship work.

Hooking her toes in the waistband of

his boxers, Savannah pushed them the rest of the way down his legs. She nibbled at his chin. "Logan, stop thinking and kiss me."

He nestled into her neck and breathed in the fragrance of her perfume. <u>Happy</u> she'd called it. The fresh scent fit her, the way she was always so up and vivacious, at least when her mother wasn't pressuring her.

The phone ringing penetrated his haze. Whoever it was, they could call back. He covered Savannah's mouth with his and closed his eyes. She tasted like the beer they'd shared, half of which sat abandoned on the bedside table. The last thing he wanted was alcohol to lull any part of tonight.

The ringing stopped and he relaxed and got back to the task at hand, making love to the beautiful woman in his bed. He'd gotten no more than two kisses when his cell rang. The caller was insistent, but not as insistent as Savannah's searching mouth.

She paused for a breath. "Think you should answer that?"

"No." He moved one hand up and fondled her breast. "I don't have that many friends. They can call back."

She combed his hair out of his face and pushed up for another kiss. "They called both phones."

Resting his forehead against the pillow, he grinned, then shoved himself off Savannah and grabbed his cell. "It's my mom. Let me just make sure everything's okay. Keep that position."

"I'll be here." She stretched like one of those models in a mattress ad. He stared at her bare breasts. An X-rated mattress ad.

He propped himself on the pillow and hit redial, noticing that Casper didn't seem the least bit concerned by anything going on around him. The dog had curled up on the old comforter he'd put in the corner for him. Three chew toys lay beside the makeshift bed and the dog appeared to be dreaming as his front feet kept jerking. Strange creature. But he seemed to have adopted them. And as of yet, nobody had answered the fliers Savannah distributed.

"Hi, sweetie. Just checking to make sure you're coming for Thanksgiving," Mom said.

Fighting a groan, Logan searched for an excuse. "Hi, Mom. Look, I'm swamped right now with work, and final semester, and getting all the papers turned in so I graduate."

"You have to eat and I can't believe college would have anything going on Thanksgiving Day," she said, shooting down his excuses. "Dad promised to behave."

"Like we haven't heard that before. He'll be an ass, as usual." Logan closed his eyes. "I'm seeing someone. Thought we'd just spend a quiet day together."

"Bring her. We'd love to meet her." His mother sounded way too delighted.

Savannah ran her hand up his chest and whispered. "You should be with your family."

No, he shouldn't. Home was the last place he should be. "You willing to go with me?" he mouthed.

She didn't respond, but he figured she had to get to know them at some point.

"We'll be there." He widened his eyes at Savannah as he hung up. "If I have to suffer through dinner, you're not getting off the hook."

Savannah clutched the sheet to her breast. "Is your mom okay with me coming?"

"Are you kidding? I'm finally bringing a date home. She's elated. Not her I'm worried about."

"Trust me. Coming from someone who no longer has a father, you should make peace with yours."

"You think your family is dysfunctional?" Logan scoffed. "Your father loved you. My old man will use anything within his twisted mind to make the day miserable for me, for Mom, for everyone. It's his freakin' passion."

Chapter Seventeen

Despite the past five glorious nights in Logan's bed, Savannah had reservations about spending Thanksgiving at his parents' house. She rubbed her sweaty palms down her black slacks. "Am I dressed okay?"

"As long as you have on clothes my mom won't even notice."

"Bet she never missed the first half of your chorus recital because she saw another lady wearing the same outfit and insisted on going home to change, huh?"

"Nope. Mom would have been there smiling. Wearing her lab coat because she had to rush back to the pharmacy." Logan flashed a wry grin. "My old man, on the other hand, didn't even make it to my high school graduation."

She remembered Logan's father as one of those stocky men who could crush rocks with his bare hands. "I'm not going to get along with him."

He winked. "One more thing we have in common."

He pulled up to the curb in front of the house and squeezed her hand. "We smile. We eat. We leave."

Savannah took in a breath and looked around the neighborhood. She'd only been here once and that was back when they were dating the first time. Small frame houses. Single car garages, many of which had been enclosed for more living space.

Logan came around and opened the truck door, then gave her a long kiss. "They won't bite."

Smiling, she straightened her burgundy blouse, slipped her arms into her silk brocade jacket, and grabbed her purse and two bottles of wine.

Colorful leaves swirled across the yards and rustled down the street from the brisk wind. Smoke puffed from the chimney, the woodsy scent reminding her of helping Daddy haul in wood and build a fire on the first cold night of the season.

Logan pulled a brown grocery bag from behind the seat. "They always make me bring olives, pickles, and cranberry sauce." He grinned. "One would surmise they don't have proper appreciation for my culinary talents."

A teenage boy darted down the car-lined street, sprang into the air, and caught a football on the rebound as it bounced off the pickup. "Sorry."

Logan glanced at the windshield where it had hit. "No problem."

When Logan opened the front door, aromas of roasting turkey and fruit pies engulfed them and sounds of the Macy's Parade and a marching band squawked from the television. Logan squeezed Savannah's hand.

　　Logan's brother bounded up from the sofa as if grasping for any diversion. "Hey, Savannah." Dale gave her a wink and shoved his older brother. "Yeah, like I didn't guess something was up that day at the lake."

　　Mr. Reid nodded from his seat in the recliner, then buried his face back in the newspaper.

　　Kat stuck her head around the kitchen door, recognized Savannah, and squealed. "All right!" She wrapped an arm around her shoulder and waved a wooden spoon at Logan. "Make yourself useful and put her purse and jacket in my old room."

　　Dutifully, he exchanged the grocery bag of olives and pickles for Savannah's stuff and gave her a push toward the kitchen.

　　Stepping into Mrs. Reid's country blue kitchen was like losing decades. Wallpaper with pictures of teakettles covered the walls. A small white painted breakfast table and white and blue vinyl floor. A little faded, but clean and homey. Any second she expected Donna Reed, interesting name, to stroll through the door dressed in pearls, heels, and a frilly apron.

　　Mrs. Reid had her hands in a mixing bowl of stuffing, but offered a warm smile. "Hello."

　　"Mom, this is Savannah Holt. She makes Logan smile and is going to make my house gorgeous."

"Welcome, Savannah."

"Kat, find the corkscrew. Pour me a glass of that wine." Nathan chopped an orange over a yellow plastic bowl. "So Logan conned you into joining us?"

"He assured me you were cooking." Savannah swallowed her words. Great! While attempting to compliment Nathan, she'd insulted Logan's mother's cooking, which she'd never even tasted.

Savannah started to apologize, but Mrs. Reid didn't seem to notice. Best not to call further attention to her blunder.

Nathan grinned and turned his attention to the sink piled high with fruit just as Logan returned. Savannah placed the bag of jars and cans on the floor. "What can I do to help?"

Dale nudged Logan's shoulder. "Got time to take a look at the Mustang? Something under the hood is squealing."

"You okay?" Logan asked Savannah.

"We're not going to kidnap her or lock her in the dungeon," Kat said, giving him a shove.

Logan raised an eyebrow at Savannah, but she motioned him out the door. She was comfortable with Kat and Nathan. The Reids however, not so much. They didn't seem to belong together. Hopefully the wine would relax the atmosphere.

"This should work for the olives." Kat placed a divided crystal dish on the bar. "Did Logan tell you our news?"

Savannah opened the jar and, utilizing the tiny space available on the counter, started arranging olives and pickles on the dish. "What news?"

"That you just got an extension on your contract."

Unsure what Kat was trying to say, she shrugged.

"You get to help design our nursery," Nathan said, giving Kat a hug and a kiss on the cheek.

"Oh man, congratulations." Savannah hugged Kat. "When are you due?"

"Late June." Nathan said, returning to the fruit salad.

"I can't believe Logan didn't tell me something this important."

"I wanted to tell you," Kat admitted. "I wanted to see your face."

"Well, I can't believe I'm going to have a grandchild," Mrs. Reid said, beaming from ear to ear.

Savannah inhaled the wonderful aromas. Though Nathan was a professional chef, the only sign of a gourmet dish was the chocolate soufflé. Just good old-fashioned home cooking. Fresh vegetables in blue ceramic bowls and hot baked rolls. The smell of yeast alone was enough to pack five pounds on Savannah's backside. No similarity to the culinary recipes her mother spent hours and fortunes concocting. Neither were there sterling silver serving dishes or imported china like Mom used to impress her guests.

Partners By Design

Constance Holt might not have a formal education, but she'd mastered every art of entertaining. Beauty. Style. Cooking. Treating friends and associates to lavish dinner experiences.

Savannah sat next to Logan and tried to enjoy the wonderful home cooked meal, but the awkward silence had her so jumpy she could barely swallow. Dale scooped food in so fast he couldn't possibly chew before swallowing. Kat and Nathan, bless their hearts, made a couple stabs at small talk, but nobody responded. Everyone had a glass of wine, except Mr. Reid who'd brought a brown beer bottle to the table.

Savannah swallowed and took a shot at helping Kat and Nathan lift the mood. "I don't remember the last time I had fresh green beans. They're delicious."

"We're so happy you could join us, dear. Is your family local?" Mrs. Reid asked.

"My mom is spending today with my sister and her in-laws in Dallas." She and her mother hadn't spoken since the morning Constance had pitched her fit. Mom refused to even answer her calls. Still, Savannah was relieved Constance wasn't alone today.

Logan flashed Savannah a grin, then returned his focus to his plate and continued to take bite after bite. She replayed his words in her mind. 'We smile, we eat, we leave.'

"You hanging around for the Cowboys game?" Dale asked, shoveling the last bite

Partners By Design

in and laying his fork on his plate.

"Not today. We..."

Mr. Reid interrupted. "Your brother is too good to hang out with us for more than the mandatory meal."

Logan nodded toward his mother. "It's Thanksgiving. Don't ruin it for her."

Mrs. Reid twisted her hands and forced a smile. "Karl, we have a guest."

Savannah felt his father's gaze skim her torso as if he loathed every inch of her. "He just brought her along for an excuse to rush off after lunch."

"Go figure. You always make it so pleasant," Dale said.

Savannah flinched at the hostility. Her family had their issues, but things didn't get rude at holiday dinners. Everyone was genteel enough to at least keep up a façade.

Kat started to speak, but Mr. Reid cut her off and focused on Logan. "Admit it. You only brought this socialite to Thanksgiving in her fancy clothes and expensive perfume so you could prove how much better than us you think you are. Think all that education makes you superior?"

"Karl." Mrs. Reid's voice trembled.

Logan laid his fork down and stood. "Savannah, are you ready?"

Mr. Reid's chair scratched against the linoleum as he struggled to his feet. "So now you aren't even staying to finish dinner?"

Dale stood. "Dad, leave him alone. Why do you always try to make everything his fault?"

Neither Logan nor his father acknowledged Dale had even spoken.

Savannah wasn't sure what to do. Sit and practice being invisible?

Logan leveled a cold stare on his father. "I don't have to listen to this and Savannah certainly doesn't. She hasn't done anything to you."

Mr. Reid's fists clenched at his side. "She'll blow through every red cent you earn. And when that runs out, she'll move on to the next mark. Serves you right."

Logan stepped up into his face, nose to nose. "You don't know any more about her now than you did before. She's worked just as hard for her education, her business, as I have."

Savannah held her breath with the rest of the family as his father's wild animal gaze burned into Logan.

"You telling me she's that girl from high school?" Mr. Reid harrumphed. "Just because she let you sow a few teenage oats back then don't mean you have to let her trash everything you've worked your ass off for."

Tears stung the back of Savannah's eyes. For the first time she experienced firsthand how Mom felt facing unfair ridicule. Karl Reid's cutting words were reverse snobbery, but snobbery all the same. She started to stand, but Kat grabbed her hand and shook her head. Should she call a cab? Make a discreet exit?

Logan didn't budge. "Listen, old man. I've been making my own decisions since you kicked me out and I'm not listening to your bullshit now. You're drunk and you're out of line."

Navy blue eyes challenged navy blue. "And you know I'm right," Mr. Reid said.

"I know you're a miserable person on a mission to bring the rest of this family down to your level."

Every drop of blood drained out of Mr. Reid's face.

Savannah held her breath.

The older man turned and lumbered across the room like a worn down prizefighter. He kicked the back door open and charged down the back stoop.

The slamming wood broke the intense silence.

Logan stood, hands on hips, staring at the ceiling. Mrs. Reid's face matched the eggshell tablecloth. Kat's eyes were huge as she exchanged glances with Nathan.

The clock ticked. The refrigerator whirred. Savannah swore she heard the oven pop as it cooled. Awkward tension hung as heavy as the storm clouds rolling in from the west.

Savannah did not belong here. This

was a family ordeal and she was not family. Although it seemed, she'd unknowingly made her mark years earlier.

Logan gritted his teeth. "I'm sorry." He retrieved their jackets from the back bedroom and wrapped his arms around his mother. "I love you. Sorry about dinner."

She squeezed him tight, as if she didn't want to turn loose. "I love you too. But you aren't the one who should apologize."

"Thanks for having me." Savannah gave Mrs. Reid a gentle hug and offered a hesitant grin at Kat and Nathan before following Logan to the truck.

She pictured the little red Miata she'd parked at the front curb and how young she and Logan must have looked. They'd been no more than kids. But Logan had possessed maturity beyond other boys. That had been part of what attracted her.

The lines around his mouth were tense as he pulled away from the house. "That won't happen again."

She turned, taken back by his abruptness and lead foot as he tore out of the neighborhood. As bad as the confrontation had been, she wanted to point out any positive. "He's obviously proud of what you've accomplished. Looking out for you."

"That's one take on it." He accelerated onto the freeway and shifted into third.

"At least he wants what's best for

you. Supports your decision to go to college and how hard you've worked for your degree."

Logan's jaw jutted out. "The only decision he ever supported was when I told him I didn't need anything from him."

She softened her voice, not certain he'd answer. "Sounds like he singles you out?"

No response.

"I'm a good listener," she said.

A headshake, but no words.

"Exciting about Kat's pregnancy," she said, making one last effort to lighten the mood.

"Yeah, Nathan will be a good dad."

She gave up and sat in her seat. Maybe she should give him space. Non-stop togetherness this soon in the relationship was too much, overload. They weren't ready for today.

As soon as he opened the apartment door, Savannah started stuffing her clothes, makeup, and toothbrush into her bag. "You know what? I think I'll just go on home. I should call Chelsea. Wish them a Happy Thanksgiving. See if Mom is speaking to me yet."

He tossed his keys and jacket on the bed. "Whatever you want to do."

Partners By Design

Chapter Eighteen

Savannah opened her eyes with a start. What was that? Maybe she'd been dreaming? Holding her breath, she detected a distinct click against her bedroom window. The room was pitch dark except the clock face which read three-forty-five AM. She eased up to the side of the bed, lifted one mini blind slat, and peered out just as another pellet hit the window.

Logan stood in the center of the front lawn, arm drawn back, poised to toss the next pebble. The fog and drizzle surrounded him in an eerie mist.

He hadn't made the slightest effort to stop her from leaving his apartment the evening before and now he was standing on her lawn in the rain? She'd lain awake until two hours ago trying to figure out how to draw him out. How to get him to talk about whatever was eating away at him. He could dish out grief to her about her issues, yet the more upset he was over his, the deeper he burrowed into his silent, brooding cave.

Another pebble hit the window and she couldn't chase away the giddy teenage rush, remembering a similar episode when they'd slipped out in the middle of the night to drive to the park and make-out.

Partners By Design

She'd no more than gotten back through the window and into bed before her parents' alarm clock went off.

Only tonight, a funny wire-haired dog sat at Logan's feet as if offering his support in the mission.

Tapping on the window, she motioned Logan toward the front door.

She belted her heavy terry robe and padded barefoot across the cold, wood, living room floor. The temperature had dropped overnight. In an effort to economize, she hadn't turned the heat up.

The chill fit her mood anyway.

She struggled with the safety chain, then the deadbolt, and swung the door open.

"Still speaking to me?" he asked with a shy grin.

"I'm not the one who doesn't speak." Her eyes swallowed him up as he stepped inside. Soft, faded jeans, snowy white tee shirt, and brown leather jacket.

He pulled a long stemmed red rose from behind his back and held it out.

Ohmygod. Her frustration melted away and she tried to keep her hand steady as she accepted the flawless token. Never, ever, in her whole entire life had anyone gotten to her the way Logan Reid did.

"Sorry I shut you out last night." He shrugged out of the jacket and tossed it onto the sofa then ran his thumb across her lips. "I'd hoped Thanksgiving wouldn't be that bad. The last thing I wanted was to subject you to my drunken father."

"A wise man recently reminded me that we aren't responsible for our parents." She wrapped her arms around his neck and stared into the stormy blue depth of his eyes. "I'm just not used to people who don't talk."

"That's because females monopolized your house." He rubbed his nose against hers and moved in for a kiss. "I promise, I won't put you through one of my family fiascos again or allow my father to insult you."

Flexing her neck, she closed her eyes. "Are we crazy to even think this can work between us?"

"It can work." His sturdy arms and hot-blooded kisses were almost enough to convince her. "We're too hard headed to not make it work."

She took his hand. "It's warmer in bed."

He tugged back on her hand, but didn't budge. "We need to talk and I'm not sure how well that would work snuggled in soft sheets."

Whoa. She tightened the belt on her robe. "Let me turn the heat up and then I'll make coffee. If you're hungry, we have some leftover cinnamon streusel Mallory made before she headed out Wednesday."

"I'll start the coffee."

Not even waiting for a pat, Casper

curled up on the overstuffed cushion Savannah had bought for him and let out a deep sigh. He seemed a bit put out that they were interrupting his night's sleep.

Logan filled the coffee pot while she turned up the heat and scrounged a bud vase from the cabinet.

She placed the rose and vase on the drop leaf table, then popped two slices of cinnamon streusel into the microwave.

Logan watched the slow dripping coffee like a starving man. "You know, one of us should learn to cook."

"I'll check into cooking classes." She wrinkled her nose. "We can learn together."

"After graduation."

"We could starve before then." Savannah placed two empty mugs on the counter and sat across from Logan. In her heart she knew they weren't true, but his father's words still bothered her. "Am I an anchor around your future, your business?"

"Don't!" Logan fought to stay cool. He had to explain, but it wasn't easy to talk about his father. "My old man doesn't understand anymore about this--" He pointed from her to him. "--what's going on between us, than your mother does. It's our lives."

"I know. And I know I love you. But if you don't talk to me, how can I help?"

She reached to touch him, but he stiffened. She dropped her hand.

He grabbed her hand and squeezed. "I know."

"You got in a fist fight with your father and left home because of me? He threw you out because I was too young?"

He'd thought he was past all this. Past the empty hole inside him. "My relationship with dear old dad stunk way before that night. I already had a plan. I just put it into action a few weeks early."

"How did he know we were having sex?" She frowned. "Or that I was only sixteen?"

Hopefully she'd never discover the answer to those questions. He forced his fists to unclench and got up to pour the coffee. He shrugged. "What does that matter now? Past history."

"Maybe you should deal with this. Get closure." Savannah came up behind him and rested her face against his back.

He fought hard not to jerk away. Very many more questions and she'd figure out the whole story.

"You were just a kid too, Logan. We were both in high school. What happened between us was stronger than we knew how to handle. I don't think an entire army could have kept us apart."

Maybe not, but her mother sure as hell had.

He set the mugs on the table while

Savannah placed the coffee cake on plates and grabbed a couple forks. "So why is your father so determined to make your life hell?"

Logan stretched his legs out in front of him and took a sip of the steaming coffee. "I asked Mom that once, one of those nights I came home late and he took a swing at me."

Savannah didn't speak, but the tears in her eyes told him how she felt and gave him the courage to finish. He'd never admitted to anyone how bad it had been. "They'd been married about six months and things were going down the toilet fast when Dad came home and told her he was leaving her for another woman. Mom had just found out she was pregnant with me. He stayed."

"That's an asinine reason to abuse your child. I don't care how angry a person gets, you don't take your fist to people." She entwined her fingers in his. "Well, as much as I disagree with his methods, he succeeded in making you into your own man."

He squeezed her hand, then stood and refilled his coffee mug. "And he gave me an excellent example of what I don't want to turn into."

"Yet you've always wanted his approval?"

He closed his eyes. Was it that obvious to her when he hadn't even consciously admitted it to himself? He'd tried so damned hard just to get the guy to show up for a soccer game. Grabbing onto any crumb his old man threw out. "How sick is that? Freakin' fathers and sons."

"His concern yesterday was that I might somehow wreck what you've worked so hard for. Whether he'll admit it or not, he's proud of what you've accomplished."

One eyebrow quirked. "We tolerate each other. I don't owe him anything and he doesn't owe me anything."

She let out a breath. "At least your father doesn't try to dictate your choices."

"You give him too much credit. He didn't care what us kids did as long as we did it on our own. Mom was the one behind us."

"Were you at least close to Kat and Dale?"

He laughed. They needed to lighten up. "Yeah, just like every other big brother. Did everything in my power to make their lives miserable."

She leaned across the table and grabbed him for a kiss. "I'm serious."

"Me too!" He ran a hand inside the collar of her robe. "So serious it scares the hell out of me."

She finger-combed his hair back from his forehead. "I'm struggling, even without Mom to support. Even before Mallory bowed out. I've got to find a cheaper place to live. I won't be able to pay the rent on the office without my regular paycheck. I have school loans."

Partners By Design

"Actually, I have some of that covered."

"What covered?" She sat back and stared.

He popped a bite of sticky cinnamon bread into his mouth and gave her time to wonder.

"Are you going to tell me what you're talking about?"

"Nope, but with the right technique, I might be seduced into showing you."

"Seduced?"

"Yeah." He drained his coffee mug and wiggled the table. "This thing's not very sturdy." He came around and tugged her to her feet, his eyes still scanning the room.

"Logan?"

He untied her robe and slid his hands around her waist. He sucked in a breath and stared at her bare breasts and lower. "You forgot to put on panties."

"I like to sleep in the nude. Wasn't expecting guests."

"Could've fooled me. I thought you only slept nude with me."

"I'm not having sex until you tell me what your secret plan is."

He lifted her up on the counter and cupped her right breast, drawing her nipple into his mouth. If he played this right, he could make her forget talking.

"It's not going to work," she

whispered, but she was already arching her back and reaching for the snap on his jeans.

He kissed lower and spread her legs. She leaned against the cold tile and her eyes clouded over as she wrapped her legs around his waist.

This woman had captivated him not once but twice in a lifetime. And this time he wasn't letting her go.

* * *

"So where are we going?" Savannah asked as Logan backed the pickup out of her drive. Casper sat content on the seat between them, pink tongue lolling out and from all appearances smiling. Of course, she was grinning like a loon too, so maybe the dog was just mimicking her. The sun was up, even though it was hard to tell with the low, heavy clouds.

Logan turned on the wipers. "Patience."

"Not one of my stronger traits. Come on, tell me. I don't deal well with suspense. I can't imagine what you've come up with to pay bills."

"Do you ever hush?" he asked, but at least he said it with that sideways grin.

"There is a method to my jabbering. I figure if I drive you nuts, you'll tell me just so I'll shut up. Is it working?"

"Nope." He shifted gears. "So you know all about my sordid past. Has your mother always expected you to live her dreams?"

Savannah stuffed her hands between her knees and took a deep breath. "When my dad died, he left us in serious debt. Mostly because of my mother's desire for a more prominent social standing. His hundred-thousand dollar life insurance policy paid for an elaborate funeral and the credit cards. But it didn't leave too much to cover twenty-three years left on a thirty year mortgage, car payments, living expenses, and educating two daughters, not to mention Chelsea's lavish wedding."

"So why didn't she get a job like normal people?"

"Because she devised this plan. If she sent Chelsea and me to top universities, we'd meet the type men who could afford to support us."

"And in turn you'd support her."

Savannah shrugged. "I believe at the time she did it for us. She planned to find a rich husband of her own."

"And you bought into that?"

Savannah shrugged. "Mom doesn't even have a high school diploma."

"Really?" His eyes widened. "You'd never know it by the way she presents herself."

"She'd die if she knew I know this. But, I overheard my parents arguing once. She was working as a stripper when she met my dad." Savannah had never even told Chelsea that.

"Now that, I wouldn't have guessed."

"She's scared to death she'll end up back in that life. Not stripping, but living hand to mouth in a dump somewhere. Her birth name wasn't even Constance. It was Clementine, but she changed it when she married Dad. She told us she had no family. All she has are her looks and me and Chelsea. She works hard to maintain her appearance, but she's not twenty anymore."

He scratched his head and made a right turn. "You're tearing at my heartstrings. People age. Doesn't give her the right to expect you to fund her extravagant lifestyle. Other people find jobs and live within their means."

"My mom usually has a man around to pay the bills. Get this. Donald, the one she let move in, turned out to be just like her. They each thought the other had money." She shrugged. "In between her relationships, Chels and I help. But Jared, Chelsea's husband, cut Mom off." She looked out the window at the fog. "Whatever else was wrong with their marriage, my father loved her. The night he died, he asked me to look after Mom. Said I was the strong one. He just wanted our family to stick together." She closed her eyes and tried not to cry.

Logan pulled into the driveway of the little Tudor he'd been renovating and took her hand. "He knew you'd try to take care of things. The guy was dying and scared."

Wiping the tears out of her eyes, she forced all the disturbing thoughts to the back of her mind where they belonged. "So,

Partners By Design

we're going to work on your client's house today and he's going to give us a giant bonus?" she asked, studying the little rock bungalow.

His only answer was a sexy grin.

"Okay? I'm dense, but why are we here?"

"Our house."

She blinked and sat up straight in the seat. "What?"

"Mrs. Zimmerman got home from Australia."

Not comprehending what he was saying, she shook her head. "And?"

"Their big house hasn't sold. As beautiful and quaint as the Tudor is, she decided it was too small for her furniture. So, I offered to buy it, as is." His grin broadened. "I write off what Zimmerman owes me as a down payment and take over payments. How's that for creative financing?" He slid out, came around, and opened her door, still wearing that crooked grin.

Savannah's heart stopped. He'd bought this house for her? For them? She took his hand and followed him up the stone steps onto the covered porch. But she wasn't sure she was comfortable with being that...together...connected...dependent.

Logan opened the door, put his hand on her back, and followed her inside. Casper darted inside and started a full scale sniffing exploration of each room.

Savannah swallowed a lump in her throat. "I...I'm in shock." Blinking her eyes, she turned and studied him. "I love this house, but I don't get it. How is this going to help our finances? It's just more debt."

"Don't love it too much. We're going to flip it."

Every word he said confused her more.

"Here's the plan. We buy a house, good location, just needs renovating, a little TLC. Pick it up below market, live in it while we renovate, and resell for a hefty profit. Invest in another one and do it again."

A business partnership made her even more nervous than a physical one. "Except that takes time and we need money now."

"True, but if we renovate the bath and a bedroom and move in, the payment is about half the rent on our two current places. With our combined skills, the only cost is a few supplies and a lot of elbow grease."

He wanted to mingle both their personal and professional lives! She crossed her arms and squeezed her stomach. "And if we split up?"

Logan's eyes narrowed. "We haven't even moved in together and you're worried about splitting up?"

"Financially I'd be sunk even worse than I am now."

"You think I'd take all the money and leave you broke?" His brow creased.

She backed against the wall and stared at the half-renovated dining room. "I'm not blind. I've seen what my mom has gone through trying to make it. I won't be dependent on you."

His jaw stiffened. "You mean you don't trust me."

She didn't speak.

"Savannah, once I commited to you, I'm all in."

"And what about last time?" She stared him in the eye and waited for a response. She understood they had been teens and about the jailbait thing, but the hurt and fear from his abandonment still wasn't resolved.

"So for the next seventy-five years, every time we fight, you're going to throw that up in my face? I left. I'm sorry. But either you trust me, or you don't. End of story. It's called commitment."

Seventy-five years? She let that register. After a long pause, he slammed out the front door. Her body trembled. He could destroy her. Almost had. But he wouldn't have had the ability to do that if she hadn't been so in love with him.

Mallory'd been right. She either had to trust Logan or break off the relationship. And after finding him again, living without Logan wasn't an option.

As she stepped out onto the porch, she found Logan standing at the rail, his back to her, staring across the yard. She slipped her hand in his. Finally she worked up the courage to break the tense silence. "I love you. We're going to make this work together. As partners. Fifty-fifty."

"How about I go fifty-one?" He squeezed her hand. "I love you too, Savannah."

She exploded with love and hope. "Then I'll give fifty-two." She took his hand and led him back inside.

Savannah wandered through the empty house with a new perspective. She was still nervous, but optimistic. Probably because he filled every need. Physical, no doubt. Emotional, they were getting there. Financial. She sucked in a breath.

She was thrilled with both his innovative plan and the fact that he was including her in his long-term future. Apparently, Logan had no doubts.

She surveyed the empty master bedroom and little rock fireplace where Casper was now sniffing. "You think we can pull this off and afford to keep the office? I mean, you'll lose the income you were planning on from this job."

"That's the best part. I won't. Zimmerman's existing house hasn't sold. Dated. Not enough natural light. He asked me to give him a bid on what it would take to open it up, add a couple skylights, knock out a wall, replace windows, and modernize the exterior."

"Is this what you want to do for a living?"

Logan rolled a nail with the toe of his boot. "It'll do until I get established. Get some money coming in. If we work our asses off and aren't extravagant for awhile, we'll get both businesses going and have the money to branch out."

For the first time, Savannah dared hope things might work. She loved Logan and he loved her. She knew that as well as she knew they'd loved each other in high school. What she had to get past was the memory that their love hadn't been enough to keep him from leaving her.

Partners By Design

Chapter Nineteen

Logan got out of the truck, adjusted his shirt collar, and straightened his back. As much as he dreaded this confrontation, he had to make peace with Constance Holt.

Like that was going to happen.

But if they could at least reach a truce. Agree to pretend not to despise each other, for Savannah's benefit. He and Savannah didn't have a chance with Constance holding the past over his head.

When he'd called Savannah's mother, she'd agreed they needed to talk, but still she made him wait two minutes on the stoop. Power play.

The door opened and her gaze scaled him. Without a word, she turned and traipsed into the living room, leaving him a seductive view of tight brocade pants and black sweater. She waved her hand. "Have a seat."

He kept his stance. "You and I need to reach an understanding. We both love Savannah and the last thing either of us wants is to hurt her."

Pouring a glass of wine, she stalled then turned and held it out to him.

Logan shook his head.

"I'd rather see her hurt in the short run than ruin her entire life." Constance took a sophisticated sip.

"Not your choice."

Green eyes widened and the corners of her glossy lips turned up. "Yes, it is and you know it or you wouldn't be here."

Downing half the glass, she nailed him with a menacing cat-eyed glare. "I've brought her this far and I will do whatever it takes to insure her future."

He flinched as a muscle in his neck stretched taut. "Don't threaten me."

"And you believe your love stands a chance in Hell if I tell her?" Constance scoffed.

"I'll take my chances." He shifted his weight to the other foot and shoved his hand in his pocket to keep from rubbing his neck. "Why can't you just be happy for her like a normal mother? You know she's in love with me just like you knew it the first time around or you wouldn't have done what you did."

She took a deep breath. "It wasn't enough that you stole a sixteen year old girl's innocence? Now you've destroyed her chances with a man who already has ten times more money than you can make in a lifetime."

"She doesn't love Truesdale." He paused. "But she loves you. Would you destroy your relationship with your daughter just to keep her away from me?"

"I'm her mother. In time she'll get over it. But believe me, Mr. Reid. I will tell her."

He gritted his teeth. "Not if I tell her first."

She flashed a self-confident smirk. "Then why haven't you, hmm? Why haven't you just come right out and told Savannah the sordid truth?"

Taking a couple steps toward her, he had the satisfaction of making her step back. "Because no matter how deep my hatred of you, I love Savannah more."

Logan turned and somehow made it to the truck without looking back. He didn't think Constance would tell Savannah, but he couldn't afford the risk. The tightrope. Always wondering if today would be the day. He didn't want anything between him and Savannah. The only choice was to come clean and hope her love was strong enough to understand. To forgive him.

His ringing cell phone interrupted his thoughts. "I need you to stop by the downtown site and make sure all the pipes are wrapped and winterized," his boss said. "The weather report is predicting mid-teens and sleet within the next two hours."

The wind had already shifted from the north and the trees twisted and crackled in the cold. "I'll run by. Already secured the site on Summit," Logan said.

"Thanks."

Logan headed toward the job site. The sooner he took care of this, the sooner he could get to Savannah. There was no easy way to come clean with her, but a warm fire and a bottle of wine in the Tudor sounded like a good start.

Maybe two bottles.

He was almost to the jobsite when the cell phone rang again. Sometimes technology could be a pain. "This is Logan."

"Hi," his mom said.

"Hey." Her voice sounded different. Something was up. "Everything okay?"

Tiny sleet pellets bounced off the hood of the truck as Logan parked in front of the construction site. He could hear her breathing, but she waited a long time before she spoke. "I'm calling to extend an invitation to you and Savannah for Christmas."

"Mom, I love you, but I'm not putting her through that again."

"I changed the locks this time. I've hired a lawyer. He's not coming back. I want us to be a family."

Whoa. Leaning back, Logan gave the conversation his full attention. "We are a family, whether you stay with Dad or not. Don't do this because of Thanksgiving."

"Have you thought how we must have looked to Savannah? I am doing what I should have done, wanted to do years ago. There is no reason to put any of us through this any longer. Even your father will be happier. All three of you kids are grown now. I have no excuse to put this off."

Logan and Kat had tried to talk Mom into leaving him every time one of these incidents happened. But they'd never thought she'd do it. "Okay. But like you said, we're all grown. You have to make the decision that's right for you. "

"I have. And he's fine. He's at Uncle Hal's."

At least he was at his brother's house and not out on the street. "Good. Mom, I need to check with Savannah about Christmas. This is our first Christmas together, but I promise we'll be over during the holidays at some point. But right now, the storms moving in and I'm late getting to her house. I gotta go." Constance wouldn't come out in this weather and he didn't think she'd tell Savannah over the phone, but instinct said he needed to get to Savannah as soon as possible.

"Apologize to her for me, please."

"I will," Logan assured her.

"Go get your girl." He could almost hear the smile in his mother's voice.

* * *

Savannah wrapped a plate in a dishtowel and placed it in the box on the kitchen table, then reached for the next dish. Darn this weather. It was taking Logan so long she might have the entire kitchen packed before he arrived. They

Partners By Design

planned to haul a load of boxes to the Tudor, build a fire, and cuddle up for the duration.

She stretched and turned up the radio as the forecast came on. "Temperatures plummeting to single digits by morning." However, now they were predicting that instead of the moisture staying north, the metroplex could end up with up to two inches of ice.

"Savannah, are you here?" Constance strolled into the kitchen as if the last time they'd spoken she hadn't practically disowned her as a daughter.

Mom ran her hand over the spool cabinet. "That's a nice piece." She looked around at the half-filled boxes. "What on earth are you doing?"

Savannah shouldn't have left the door unlocked for Logan. Placing the dish into the box, she glanced at the opulent fur collar on Mom's off white sweater. "Packing."

Constance's lips thinned and her boot clad foot tapped against the wood floor. "You aren't moving in with Logan?"

"I love him. Why shouldn't we share a place, save on living expenses? More money for the business."

Mom sat down in a kitchen chair and rubbed her eyes that way she did without actually touching them. Her rose-shaded eyelids closed as she sighed. "I'd so hoped to spare you this."

Savannah's arms bristled with chill bumps. Mom and melodrama--good indication Savannah wasn't going to like what she was about to hear. "Then spare me."

"You should sit down." Mom moved a stack of cookbooks off the chair next to hers and patted the cushion. "I need your full attention."

Oh, this sounded more ominous by the syllable. Savannah sat. "Okay."

Constance fidgeted, stared into Savannah's eyes, and then looked away. She squeezed Savannah's hand, dropped it on the table, only to pick it up again. "I couldn't tell you this before, but you're older now. And it's important that you know what kind of man you're in love with."

"I do know him, Mother." Savannah set her jaw and ignored the massive lump in her throat. "Better than you do."

"Are you sure?"

Savannah jutted her chin but the lump in her throat restricted her next breath.

"When you and Logan dated in high school, he..." Mom dropped Savannah's hand and rubbed up and down her own arms. "Remember the night I invited him to dinner and I told you he didn't show up? Well, he showed up before you got home."

Savannah swallowed and fought the dread that crept into her mind. "But you said..."

"I know. I lied. But I couldn't stand to see you hurt by the truth. I guess I was embarrassed, felt a little responsible. After all, I was the adult." She looked away. "He came on to me. Shoved me up against the wall and tried to..."

The world stopped turning and crumbled around Savannah like shattered shards of glass. Her Logan? Logan who'd made wild and tender love to her all afternoon on Sunday, had seduced her mother on Monday? Tears stung her eyes, but refused to fall. "I don't believe you."

"Sweetheart, why would I make something this sordid up?"

Savannah stared at her gorgeous mother and tried to tell herself this couldn't be true. But she knew better. That's what he'd been hiding from her all this time? Refusing to talk about?

Savannah's stomach filled with raw bile. "I have to know exactly what happened."

As Logan pulled up in front of Savannah's house and recognized the Cadillac, his heart stopped dead. He was too late. Only one thing would have brought Constance Holt out in this weather.

He bailed out of the truck, turned up his collar against the stinging sleet and ran for the cover of the porch.

He opened the front door and burst into Savannah's living room. Maybe Constance hadn't told her. "So much for

Partners By Design

the worst of this going north. The roads are--"

The room was warm, but Savannah's expression was more frigid than the sleet. "You slept with me one night and tried to have sex with my mother the next?"

Her accusation slammed into his chest.

Constance stood in the kitchen doorway, staring at him with the triumphant glow of victory.

He'd never hated another human being with the intensity he hated Constance Holt. "I did not try to have sex with your mother."

Savannah paced across the room, putting distance between them, then spun to face him. "Really? So she just made it up that you kissed her, shoved your hand up her blouse and...?"

Constance had decided being rid of him was worth destroying her daughter. If the woman was vicious enough to hurt her this deeply with lies, then she'd just become a much more formidable enemy. He reached out a hand. "Savannah."

"So that's my answer?" Savannah's eyes blazed into his. "You aren't denying it."

"Would it do any good?" Logan met her eyes, but all he found was fury and hatred.

"I was in love with you." Savannah's voice cracked.

"I loved you then and I love you now. And your mother damn well knew it or she wouldn't have set me up that night. Tried to seduce me just to put a wedge between us."

"My mom held my hand and consoled me after you dumped me. She hated you for breaking my heart."

"What about my heart? She came on to me! The whole seduction act was blackmail to ensure that I left and stayed gone. If I'd have come near you, she'd have destroyed you. And if by some miracle you did believe me, she'd have called the cops and filed charges. We didn't have a chance."

"Lies! I see the guilt on your face!"

Logan tossed his jacket on the table by the door as his initial shock turned to white hot fury.

Constance sidled forward. "Logan, the truth's out. No need to pretend innocence."

"*You* shoved *me* up against the wall, lady!"

"You responded quite impressively if memory serves." She smiled.

Sleet clicked against the window and the nightmare that the three of them could be stranded here together spurred him into action. "I was eighteen. And my girlfriend's mother had her tongue wrapped around my tonsils." He took a deep breath. "I was too shocked to even move."

"You may have been eighteen, but you knew what you wanted." As Constance spoke, she walked toward him. "Pretty intense necking session for someone in shock."

"I...you scared the hell out of me." He backed away, but when his back hit the wall, cold fear raced through his veins. Just as it had that night. He felt his face heat, but he wasn't a traumatized teen this time. He took a step forward. "I came over that night prepared for an awkward dinner with my girlfriend's parents, not to have her mother act like Mrs. Robinson."

"Mother?" Savannah's anguished voice croaked out the words. "Did you?"

Constance turned away from Logan and reached for her, but Savannah knocked her hand away. "Of course not!"

One look at Savannah's pale, shock-ridden face and Logan knew she believed him. And her mother saw it too. It was all over now. The truth had won out, but it was a hollow victory.

"Honey." Constance dropped her hand but tilted her head to remain in Savannah's focus. "I had to make sure he didn't ever come back. I had to save you."

Savannah backed toward the door and closed her fingers around Logan's leather jacket. As badly as Logan wanted to hold her, he didn't dare move.

"Save me? From a man who loved me? A man I loved with everything new and exciting inside me? You listened to me cry myself to sleep night after miserable night knowing what you'd done."

For the first time, he recognized fear in Constance's emerald green eyes. She'd misjudged the impact this would have on Savannah. Her voice softened. "Honey, listen to me. It wasn't like you think."

Savannah's entire body trembled and tears streamed down her cheeks. "My own mother seduced my boyfriend!"

The woman turned pale. She was beaten and she knew it, but she wouldn't give up. "Savannah, he didn't love you. He was a hormonal teenage boy. He just wanted sex and once he got it--"

The heavy door banged against the wall and Logan turned in time to see Savannah run down the steps. So focused on Constance, it hadn't registered that Savannah was on the move.

Dammit. His keys were in that jacket.

"You made me do this." Constance shook her hair back and glared at him. "You've destroyed my daughter's life just like I knew you would the first time I saw you."

He had to catch Savannah. Pushing past Constance, he bolted for the door. "No, your sick little game blew up and I'm not taking the heat this time."

He raced down the icy sidewalk as the truck roared to life. He reached the curb just in time to slap the fender before the truck fishtailed on the thin sheet of freezing drizzle and tore away.

Partners By Design

"Savannah!"

Partners By Design

Chapter Twenty

The pearl white caddie loomed like a giant roadblock at the end of the narrow drive, blocking Savannah's van. Logan raced back to the house, but the door was locked. "Open the damn door, Constance!"

Nothing. No sound.

"I'll kick it in!"

He held his breath until the door creaked open. Constance's face was streaked red and brown with tears and makeup, but he had no sympathy.

"I need your car keys."

"What?" She looked right through him, almost disoriented.

"Give-me-the keys," he repeated.

The precariousness of the situation seemed to sink in and she turned and grabbed her purse off the sofa. She dug out a leopard print key case and pressed it into his hand.

His fingers closed around it as he raced toward the car.

"Logan!"

He yanked the car door open and glanced over his shoulder. He did not have time to deal with her.

She gripped the porch railing. "I love my daughter."

He took a deep breath. "I know."

The caddie purred like a kitten as he eased it into reverse. For once he was appreciative of the heavy chunk of Detroit steel and the increased traction it offered. Wish he could say the same for his pickup. Why hadn't he blocked the drive with the truck and put the damn keys in his jeans?

Ice had already coated the street and he had no idea which way Savannah had turned.

Somehow he had to get her to stop. Freaked out and driving a pickup on ice with no weight in the backend? Sure-fire formula for landing in a ditch, or worse. Pulling his cell phone out, he prayed she'd answer. Nada. Rolled to voicemail. "Savannah, call me."

The caddie shimmied to the right and he tossed the phone into the seat and put both hands on the wheel. Hell. This was Texas. He wasn't any more experienced at driving on ice than Savannah was. "Come on, sweetheart. Talk to me," he said, his plea lost in the empty car.

Sleet covered the windshield and the wipers fought to swipe it away before it froze to the frigid glass. The radio announcer said the temp had fallen ten degrees in the past hour. Twenty-two and plunging.

If she was thinking at all, she'd go someplace safe and get off these roads. A

Partners By Design

friend maybe, but the only friend he knew was Mallory and she was in Oklahoma with Quentin this weekend.

He crept along, keeping an eye peeled for any sign of his truck. There were only two places he could think of that she might have gone. The office or the Tudor. At least they were only a mile apart.

As upset as she was, he could pretty much eliminate the Tudor, since she knew he'd moved the bulk of his stuff in. After Constance, he was the next to last person she wanted to talk to right now.

He slammed his hands against the steering wheel. If anything happened to Savannah, he'd make Constance pay.

He tried Savannah's cell phone again, but she still didn't answer. Surely she had it with her or Constance would have answered. Leaving another message, he hoped to God she was at least inside someplace and out of this.

The streets were deserted. Radio stations were urging people not to drive. Another hour and it'd be dark. The roads were already turning to black ice. Even the heavy Cadillac was struggling to maintain traction as he made the last blocks before the office.

He rounded the corner and almost slid the Caddie into the front end of his pickup. He blinked. The truck was sitting at an awkward angle, headed the wrong direction, and partially blocking the eastbound lane. He crept to a stop and got out. The truck windows were coated in a frosted sheet of frozen sleet and it was hard to see in, but the driver door was unlocked. No sign of Savannah. Or his keys.

He rubbed his hands up and down his arms trying to build friction, but his sweatshirt offered little protection from the biting cold. Bending down, he checked under the truck. Axle looked ok, but when she'd spun and hit, the rear tire had rolled off the rim and the curb had taken a chunk out of the steel wheel. Couldn't deal with that now. He had to find Savannah.

He gathered his laptop and tools out of the truck and crawled back in the Caddie.

When he got to the office, he found the main door locked and the building deserted. Savannah had his keys so he couldn't get in to check. He dialed the office phone. If she was there, she still wasn't ready to talk.

He stepped back and looked up at their office windows, but there were no lights on. Sleet peppered down the collar of his sweatshirt and melted against the heat of his skin. The thick cotton was fast becoming soaked.

A coat. If he was going to find Savannah, he'd better go home first and grab a coat and gloves or his fingers were going to break off. Plus he had an extra key to the office there.

Cranking up the heat in the car, he dialed Savannah's house. Constance answered. She was stranded there as she'd called every cab company in town and none of them were operating and she couldn't find the van keys. She hadn't seen or heard from Savannah, but confirmed that her cell phone wasn't there.

So Savannah did have it. That was one positive. If she was walking in this weather, she'd call him. He grimaced. Or her mother.

Trees glistened and crackled with ice and the pavement had a treacherous sheen. The storm had blown in with a vengeance and the predictions were getting worse with each report. Sleet mixed with heavy snow through tomorrow. Visibility stunk, but at least snow might help traction.

Where the hell was Savannah? Creeping along, he scanned both sides of the road for her. At this pace, it would take fifteen minutes to cover the mile home. The city had turned into an ice rink.

* * *

Savannah stood in the Tudor's master bedroom and gaped at the brass bed. The bed from Logan's grandmother's lake house. The bed they'd first made love on.

It had been made up with fresh linens and the quilt they'd bought at the fair. And logs were stacked in the little fireplace. She fought back tears as she picked up a business card and brochure off the bed. A jeweler who custom designed rings. In the midst of a maze of unpacked boxes and furniture waiting to be arranged, Logan had created a tiny utopia.

Logan was the strongest, most self-confident man she'd ever known. He wasn't easily intimidated, yet her mother had done the one thing that could shut him down.

Her heart shattered for the teenage boy she'd fallen in love with. The fear and confusion he must have felt. The humiliation on his face at Mom's squalid confession tonight.

And yet, he'd dealt with it all, was willing to keep dealing with it. For her. His words, 'It's time you stopped running from me', haunted her.

Savannah shivered and rubbed Casper's warm neck. The dog had not left her side since she'd arrived five minutes ago. He knew something was wrong and in his own funny way seemed to be trying to console her as he pressed his warm body into her hand.

Her throat was still cold and her breathing labored from her tramp through the snow. She eased out of Logan's leather jacket and wrapped it around her like his arms. Her shoulders shook and the tears fell as she sat on the old brass bed.

Betrayed by her own mother. The woman who professed to love her and promised that together they could conquer anything. The woman who had comforted her after the devastating loss that she'd purposely caused.

What kind of warped person did something like that?

It wasn't at all like Mom had told her. She'd known full well that Savannah and Logan were in love. Logan hadn't made love to Savannah then dumped her once he'd gotten what he wanted. He'd left because her mother had made sure he had no other choice.

Constance knew men. She'd brought Logan down with the one weapon in her arsenal that never failed. Her blonde bombshell sex appeal that no red-blooded male could resist.

Her mother's exquisite beauty was no blessing, but a curse.

Savannah jumped as her cell phone chimed *I Love a Rainy Night* again. She heard the front door open and waited, her gaze glued to the hallway.

The short ends of Logan's hair were spiky and dark with melted sleet and his cheeks were flushed when he stepped into the bedroom. He clicked his cell phone off, but he stopped just inside the doorway.

She stood and took a step forward, then ran her cold hand down his icy face. He was soaked. "I'm done running from you. I'm so sorry for the hell my mother put you through. I will never not trust you again."

He still didn't speak.

She pulled the wet sweatshirt over his head, then yanked the peach quilt off the bed and wrapped it around his bare shoulders. His nose and cheeks were red and his skin frozen.

His strong arms encircled her in the quilt cocoon and crushed her body against his half frozen one. They were both trembling so hard, it was difficult to tell where she stopped and he started.

"I need to explain," Logan said through chattering teeth.

"Shhh. No, you don't." Savannah put her finger to his lips. "It's over. It's just you and me now. I don't want to think about my mother or hear her name, ever again."

Logan ran a trembling hand down her cheek. "You feel that way now, but..." He tightened his arms around her. "When she gave me the car keys tonight, she wanted to make sure I knew that she loved you. She looked pretty destroyed."

"Good. Maybe I'll feel like talking to her in say... eight years."

Logan flashed that sexy, crooked smile. "As bad as I hate what she did, on some level I have to admire her creativity and determination."

"Scheming and manipulative is more how I'd describe her. I loathe that woman. I owe her nothing." Savannah traced her finger along his square jaw and stared into his stormy blue eyes. "I don't want to talk about her anymore."

His cold lips seduced hers, igniting a flicker of heat from deep inside. "Let me light the fire."

Savannah enjoyed the taste of Logan, his warmth. She pulled back and giggled.

Partners By Design

"Oh, you were talking about the one in the fireplace."

He gave her a long, sexy kiss, but just as she was getting into it, he pulled away and grabbed the matches off the mantle. "Both."

Savannah stared at the sexy seat of his tight jeans and began to believe things might work. They were going to make it.

But one issue still bothered her, one puzzle piece she couldn't fit into place. "How did your father know I was only sixteen? Someone had to tell him."

He didn't even turn. "Right."

"And nobody except my mom would have done that. But what I can't figure is how did she know the number? There are pages of Reids in the phone book and she had no way of knowing your father's name was Karl."

"She confiscated your cell phone."

Her cooling anger flared back to a boil as she realized just how calculating her mother had been. "I thought I'd lost it. She gave me a scathing lecture about responsibility and sent me back to school to find it! That's why I wasn't home when you arrived."

He raised an eyebrow. "And it severely limited my ability to contact you."

The sheer depth of the woman's treachery was still registering. She had to calm down. Her mother had maliciously

Partners By Design

stolen eight years, she wasn't going to ruin tonight. Deep breath. "How did you con Kat out of the brass bed?"

He wadded a newspaper and stuffed it beneath the logs. The fire flamed and light flickered through the darkening bedroom. "Just told her since she's now designing a nursery, if she wanted to get rid of it, I'd take it off her hands."

Savannah blushed. "So we can spend the rest of our lives loving each other in the bed we first made love in."

Casper plopped his butt in front of the fire and ignored them. The dog seemed to belong with the house as he stretched out flat of his back, paws straight up in the air and pink tongue lolled out the right side of his mouth.

Logan grinned at the dog and then slipped out of his wet jeans and socks. "Yep."

She turned back the covers, stripped out of her clothes, and dove between the sheets with Logan. "I think it was fate that Mallory rented the office from you. You planted the TCU seed in me on that long ago afternoon you drove me through the neighborhood and pointed out the project you were working on. The houses were so classy and you were full of dreams about becoming an architect."

He kissed her, rolling her over on her back. "So what are you saying?" He ran his tongue around her lips. "I'm why you decided to become an interior designer?"

Rubbing her palms up his strong back, she returned his kiss. "I never forgot. Never drove through here without keeping my eyes peeled for you." She threaded her fingers into his damp hair and kissed him hard. "Loving you started it all."

Bracketing her face with his hands, he returned her kiss, his cold lips melding with hers. She could only breathe Logan. "Savannah, my heart has been in your hand since that rainy night on your sixteenth birthday when you spun into my life in that little red convertible."

With one knee, he spread her legs and settled in between, hardly letting her talk between kisses.

She wrapped her legs around his thighs and squeezed. She wanted him here, now, and forever.

She reached between their bodies and touched him. "You are the only man I could ever imagine being in love with. No more secrets. We have to always be upfront and honest and nobody will destroy us again."

Logan cupped her bottom and moved inside her. He held her so tight she couldn't breathe. The heat from the fire hadn't had time to penetrate the room, but the heat from their bodies oozed into her bloodstream and turned ice to fire.

Partners, by design.

THE END

Partners By Design

Rocking Horse Cowboys (Available Now)

"No damn way!" Dylan McKeon blinked at the lawyer then turned his glare on his mother. "Did you instigate this?"

Daisy grinned back at him with all the innocence he knew his mother did not possess. "I'm as surprised as you, sweetie. Who'd have thought your father would do such a thing?" Judging by the upturned corners of her glossed lips, she did.

"Why would Dad leave half the ranch to Jordan?" It made no sense. Jordan had walked out of Dylan's life over two years ago and he hadn't seen neither hide nor hair of her since. Dylan turned back to the lawyer. "Is that all? What other death bed insanity did he pull?"

His father's attorney and longtime drinking buddy ran a finger down the paper and flipped the page. "A few specified items and his vast music collection he left to Daisy." He nodded to Mom. "All other personal property, vehicles, farm equipment, livestock, bank accounts go to Dylan McKeon, his only son. With the one specification."

Dylan swallowed the bile in his throat. No way in Hell he was going to allow Jordan Harris to reap a cent off of his or his father's hard work. "Fifty percent of the McKeon family's ranch? We'll see about that."

Partners By Design

ABOUT THE AUTHOR

Pamela Stone spent twenty plus years in the technology field before becoming a romance writer. She is a native Texan whose mom encouraged the importance of wardrobe, dance, and piano lessons and whose father added go-kart racing, slot cars, water skiing, and a pony to the mix. Toss in a wild imagination, lazy walks on her grandparent's farm and another grandmother with a shed full of romance novels to while away hot afternoon.

Writing is pure escapism for Pamela. Childhood imaginary friends grew into teenage fantasies. Later as a mother of two young boys, she began writing to keep in touch with the adult world. She continued writing as a method to wind down in the evenings from long days spent in Corporate America. Anybody notice a pattern here? Not enough adult socialization – write. People overload – write. Either way, she claims that writing keeps her sane. Cheaper than a therapist and tons more fun.

She still resides in Texas with her childhood sweetheart and husband. She loves writing romance and sold her first novel, Last Resort: Marriage, on Friday the 13th, June 2008. How's that for luck!

Pamela loves to hear from her readers and can be reached through her website at http://www.pamelastone.net

Made in the USA
Charleston, SC
28 June 2013